# SINBAD
## AND THE
## GOLDEN MARLIN

## HG TOWNE

Dry Diggins
Press

Published by:
Dry Diggins Press, LLC
www.drydigginspress.com

ISBN-13:  978-0692555699
ISBN-10:  0692555692

Sinbad and the Golden Marlin is also available as an ebook.

Dedicated to Ray Harryhausen


Special thanks to Schlock! Webzine and Gavin Chappell
www.schlock.co.uk

A midnight moon hung high over the Arabian Sea, casting an icy-blue luminescence down upon the mysterious island.

In the palace perched atop the isle's lone mountain, the Master meditated before the magnificent Ebon Globe. The large black sphere, its breadth about the length of a man's arm, sat upon an ornate gold-worked pedestal at the center of a large circular chamber. The dark surface of the globe was at times smooth and reflective, and at other times covered in strange pictographic reliefs or even a flickering web of energy, depending on the Master's incantations and the dark magic seething within the enigmatic object. The slowly transforming globe licked out at the Master with slight bolts of lightning, enveloping him in a gathering cocoon of evil energy until they were one in the sorcery.

Exactly how long the magician remained locked in dark conclave with the mystic orb, no one could say. Many midnights passed. Perhaps a moon, or even more. But eventually came the midnight of consummation, and whatever malevolent necromantic task he had been toiling at, it was then complete. The crackling energy womb split open like the pedals of a wicked flower, and pulled back into the surface of the Ebon Globe. The Master opened his radiant eyes...and whispered:

"Baghdad."

Zahra, daughter of Lessor Vizier Kharim Ahmadi, had long sought to become a practitioner of the black arts. Against her father's wishes, she tried to use her family's connections in the Royal Court of Baghdad to further this aim, but the only result was dishonor brought upon her family. With threats of suicide, she stilted her father's attempts to arrange marriages for her, and she continued to use every resource available, riches both monetary and womanly, in trying to coerce magicians into taking her as an apprentice. But all the mystics she could locate refused, and her pursuit of dark magic now consisted of paying men to thieve tomes and trinkets from seers, and attempting the dangerous task of deciphering the magic within the items herself.

One of the forbidden secrets Zahra gleaned from a pilfered scroll was a spell to call a demon of fire that would do one's bidding. The wicked woman fantasized about the despicable ways she could use such a servant. But the amateur magician lacked a true understanding of the spell's incantations, and she could never make the magic work. However, she was able to properly translate the instructions for arranging a room with certain objects required for the casting of the spell. It was a collection of candles, braziers, and simmering cauldrons, all arranged around a severed ram's head sitting atop a carven black stone pedestal that stood at the center of a floor emblazoned with mystic symbols.

Without the proper incantations, Zahra's uneducated attempts to invoke the necromantic power manifested themselves as a tiny, flickering light in the abysmal blackness of the darkest magic. Her tries at witchcraft caught the attentions of many creatures dwelling in the dark gulfs, but to her greatest peril, they were a bright beacon to the Master.

Born eons ago as Khur'tek Nor, the Master was an ancient wizard from a forgotten time, a power unmatched during the age in which he lived. But the faint fragments of history from those primeval days records that the magician who went by that accursed name was long ago dead and mummified.

He was the offspring of a murderer who escaped hanging and fled his people, seeking to hide from justice in forbidden, ghost-haunted ruins. In the night, the man was set upon by a demon of fire and flesh. The she-demon's body burned him with pleasure, violently fornicating with the appalling aberration of a man after taking the form of his desire, an image of lust pulled from the perverted mind of the mesmerized murderer. The demon waited until he had given his seed in one last moment of demented ecstasy before the flames that had brought him pleasure burned like hell.

Raised by the demon in her cradle of dark magic, suckled at the teat of evil, the half-breed learned well the black craft. Sent forth into the human world as an agent of chaos, destruction, and domination, the Master fulfilled every evil wish of his mother and her kind. For a millennium, he subjugated humanity through working his powerful magic, but eventually his earthly life came to an end, and he was laid to rest, not in peace, but in eternal, hellish torment.

Ages passed, and the world all but forgot the terrible deeds done by Khur'tek Nor. But some remembered. Dark forces reached out into the black gulf of death, and pulled him back, one thousand years after even his powerful black magic could not save him from being poisoned to mortal death after his one thousand years of immortal life. The fool priests that dared summon him back from night all perished in fire, and all that was theirs was then his. So began the second reign of terror perpetrated by the demon-spawned sorcerer, Khur'tek Nor.

Since his unholy resurrection, yet another thousand years had aged the world, and Khur'tek Nor had grown ever stronger. The Master was perhaps the most powerful dark magician that had ever existed whose black veins pumped with even a drop of human blood.

Atop the tall central tower of his palace, the Master called into the darkness for one of his ethereal servants. His glowing eyes sparked as he chanted, and the inhuman incantation echoed off into the moonless night sky that loomed like a cloak of evil above the mysterious island. Far below in the palace, the Ebon Globe crackled with sparks, and its surface pulsed into evil, unnatural shapes. Down out of the stars came what at first seemed a streak of darkness, a thin black cloud racing earthward from the heavens. Then it was a rolling line of dark fog above the island that twisted down toward the top of the tower where the Master waited with open arms. It continued to shrink until it became a vertical serpentine line of rolling, twisting mist that was no taller than a man. The whirlwind of mysterious dark air hovered above the tower for a moment, then twisted down and shrank once more, coalescing into a tiny, hideous imp that flapped little leathern wings as it floated down to sit on the tower's parapet. The thing was now only as tall as a man's knee, and its devilish, vaporous features seemed to shift and alter horribly from one form to another in the dim starlit night. The Master leaned down and whispered ghastly directives for evil deeds into the creature's airy, pointed ear, the thing listening intently to the commands. Then, opposite the manner in which it had arrived, the imp's form dematerialized into a twisting mist that vanished into the night sky.

Like many nights before, Zahra lay in her darkened bedchamber with the arrangement of necromantic artifacts at the foot of her bed, unaware of the perverse evil her reckless ambitions could bring down upon her.

At an open window, the air stirred, and a wisp of darkness wound down onto the sill. A moment later, the Master's servant coalesced from the compact disturbance, and noiselessly leaped down to the floor. Leering about the chamber, its pointed tail flicked back and forth in silent agitation. As it crept toward Zahra's bed, moving through the starlight and shadows, the imp's face constantly changed appearance, sometimes contorted into a countenance of nightmarish malevolence, while at other times wearing a sickening, devilish grin.

It hopped up onto the bed and began to whisper into Zahra's ear as it caressed her face. From the Master, through his servant, commandments of evil seeped into Zahra's dreams. In a trance deeper than sleep, she sighed and moaned as the ill visions poured into her. Zahra's chest heaved and her body writhed in apparent ecstasy as the Master's wishes saturated her mind.

The unholy, erotic visits from the grotesque imp continued for many moons, and with increasing frequency.

Jutting minarets dotted the nighttime skyline under the star-flecked heavens floating above Baghdad. A warm breeze scented with jasmine, palm and date blew through the summer twilight over the capital of the great Arab Empire.

In the palace of Haroun al-Rashid, Caliph of Baghdad, window shades and curtains were left wide open after another hot summer day.

In the early morning darkness, stealthy footfalls on a high ledge beneath the second-level casements went undetected in the magnificent domed palace as a shadowy figure cautiously climbed through an open window and crept across the bedchamber where the Caliph slept.

In an opulent gold-and-ivory canopy bed, the monarch lay, unaware of the intruder who had somehow evaded the patrolling guards.

Glittering on the Caliph's finger was the Star of Percepolis, a ring set with an enchanted gem said to hold the power of protection for wearers pure of heart and deed. It was the Caliph's most coveted treasure, and the jewel never left his hand.

The thief tugged off the ring, stirring its owner.

"Wha...what are *you* doing here?" the awakening Caliph mumbled. "The Star!" He tried to screech when the theft of his precious ring became apparent, but a hand muffled his cry.

The Caliph looked square at the familiar face as the man's fist slammed into his jaw, knocking the monarch unconscious.

The thief quietly slipped out of an open window, but instead of climbing down to the gardens to make good an escape from the palace grounds, the man scrambled back along the narrow ledge, ducking below the window openings as he passed them, until he reached a particular one that led into a darkened chamber, and he stealthily climbed inside.

It was the palace chamber currently assigned to Lessor Vizier Kharim Ahmadi. Inside the dimly lit room where a single candle burned, the vizier awaited the thief's return with his daughter, Zahra.

Zahra had assured her father that after they acquired the enchanted ring for the Master, the powerful magician would protect them and assist in Kharim Ahmadi's aspirations for political power. The vizier was dubious of the plan and this "master," but his greed for higher station clouded his already poor judgment. He was regrettably beholden to his devious daughter, and after the night's events, he could no longer escape from her web of lurid schemes.

"Dispel the magic immediately, lest we be caught with the impostor," Zahra commanded as she gestured toward a dark corner.

Out from behind a velvet-covered divan crept the Master's impish servant. Shunning the moonlight, the thing stayed in the shadows as it worked its magic. Suddenly, in its hand the imp held a tiny fife that materialized out of the vapors of which the imp was composed. The creature blew the pipe intently for a moment, but no sound was heard by the watchers. Instead of producing music, the playing of the fife started an unholy transformation. With wavy lines in the air surrounding him, as if looking through ripples in a clear pool of water, the handsome, bearded Arab man that had thieved the Caliph's ring was revealed to actually be a bare-faced black man, one of Zahra's slaves.

With the illusion dispelled, the imp again dematerialized, and its mist quickly streamed out of the window into the night sky.

"Can we trust him to keep this secret?" the vizier asked, looking at Zahra's slave.

"Of course we can, Father," Zahra answered as she put her hand on the thin man's shoulder. His eyes nervously darted back and forth in fear and confusion. Zahra slowly walked around the shaking slave as she spoke. "We will be assured of his silence," she uttered with soothing tone over cold malevolence.

With a movement as quick as a viper's strike, Zahra pulled her dagger and slit the man's throat. The slave clutched at his neck as he dropped, and the vizier staggered back, gasping in horror.

With strength surprising for her stature, Zahra dragged the dying man to the window and pushed him out to fall. The man's limp body tumbled from the second level of the palace, and landed with a muffled thud in the thick shrubs below.

"Are you mad?!" the vizier whispered intensely. "The guards will surely find him."

"Not until daylight, at the earliest," Zahra assured. "By then, I will be long gone with the ring, and your presence here will arouse no suspicion. As for the slave's murder— they will blame it on the criminal sailor," she reasoned confidently.

"I pray that you are right, Daughter. If your master's magic does not protect us, we'll share the sailor's fate." The idea hung in the air. "Oh, Zahra." The vizier shook his head. "I know not by what madness I let you convince me to take part in this," he lamented. "My dear daughter..."

"Yes you do, Father," she coldly interrupted. "It is the madness of your own lust for power," she sneered through her wispy veil, knowing she had him trapped like a wolf in a cage.

But, as always, Zahra had not been truthful with her father. The Master had no interest in the Caliph's ring. Zahra wished for it herself, hoping it might protect her when she finally stood in person before the Master, which she would soon do. She was bewitched by the magician, but also fearful of his great power.

The Master's true dictate, to which the vizier was oblivious, was for Zahra to abduct one of the Caliph's daughters. To this end, Zahra sent four of her female slaves to the young girl's chambers. They were instructed to wait until the palace alarm was sounded, then kidnap the princess, and flee the palace with her in the commotion that was sure to follow the theft of the Caliph's ring.

Zahra gave the slaves a special scarf that reeked of some strong acrid scent that was almost floral. It was to be placed over the mouth and nose of the princess for only a few moments, and the slaves were to be careful not to breathe the fumes themselves. After the little girl was rendered unconscious, they were to put her limp body in a large bag with the scarf, and leave the palace in the confusion. Zahra also bade them drop a curious trinket in the girl's quarters.

Zahra had just finished wiping up a few spots of her slave's blood when she heard the palace stir.

As the Caliph awoke, he tenderly felt the side of his face, trying to rub away the pain. In a moment, sleep and injury cleared from his mind and his senses returned.

"Guards!" he screamed to sound the alarm.

The Caliph knew well the man who had attacked him. As unbelievable as it was, he was sure of what he had seen.

Sinbad, the legendary sailor and captain, slumbered the deep sleep of a contented man. In his mansion on the outskirts of Baghdad, set on sprawling grounds of gardens and pavilions, he and his wives rested off a night of revelry. Family and friends had gathered at Sinbad's estate for an evening of feasting and dancing. It was a grand affair filled with joyous souls making merry with their loved ones. At one point during the festivities, Sinbad even took up his sorna horn, and joined the musicians in performing, much to the delight of his guests, as it always was. Making music with the hired minstrels was something Sinbad regularly did because, beyond being entertaining for his guests, he took great pride in being an accomplished player himself.

But all the pleasure of the night's revelry was shattered away with the palace guards' pounding on the doors of the grand entrance to his mansion. Without explanation, they roughly arrested Sinbad and led him away from his home and distraught family.

Sinbad was taken to the throne room in the palace of Baghdad. Many times before had Sinbad visited the magnificent chamber as a trusted advisor and confidant of the Caliph, but never at the rough insistence of the palace guards as he did now. But as to why he was being brought in front of the Caliph in this manner, Sinbad could only guess. It was obviously some matter of great import.

Tall pillars reached up to the grand domed ceiling of the ornately frescoed and tiled chamber. The wide colonnaded hall was lined with arched passageways leading off to the palace and out to the gardened pavilions surrounding the great structure.

At one end of the hall several stone steps led up to a low dais where Haroun al-Rashid, Caliph of Baghdad, sat upon his simple yet regal throne. Flanked by two palace guards holding large, long-handled ostrich feather fans, the Caliph scowled upon sight of his formerly trusted friend, and the tall peacock plume sticking up from behind the great jewel on the front of his turban shook with his subdued rage.

Sinbad approached the dais with his head bowed in respect, and the men of the palace court crowded in behind him to witness the happenings.

"I am honored to be in your presence, Your Majesty. What can your humble servant do for you this morning?" Sinbad asked with the customary courtly respect.

"What can you do?!" the Caliph asked in disbelief. "You have done enough already. Have you no honor? Will you offer no explanation for your wicked deeds?" The Caliph's demeanor was ripe with building anger. "I have sorely misjudged your character," he lamented, shaking his head in bewilderment.

"What has happened, my Caliph?" Sinbad asked, still oblivious to the previous night's events, and confused by the Caliph's obvious displeasure.

"I cannot bear to say these things again. They injure me

too much," the Caliph offered solemnly.   "Vizier Kharim Ahmadi has warned of your ambitions to challenge me..."

Sinbad narrowed his eyes and flashed a hostile look at Kharim Ahmadi, who had bent his head at the mention of his name.

With the Grand Vizier lying in bed, old and sick and dying, some members of the court had been underhandedly vying for favored status in the Caliph's eyes, hoping to assume the coveted position when the Grand Vizier inevitably passed.  In this chaotic atmosphere of royal court politics, Sinbad had long suspected the lessor vizier of plotting to de-throne the Caliph and install himself as ruler of the Arab Empire.

Sinbad then interrupted the Caliph, seriously violating royal protocol.

"Your Excellency, I swear on my father's grave, with Allah as my witness, I have no such ambitions!  Anyone who says otherwise spreads lies!  I am only your humble servant, my Caliph."

Gasps and murmurs rose from the gathered court nobles, the men looking back and forth at each other in disbelief at Sinbad's interruption.

"Blasphemy!" the vizier yelled piously.

"Heretic!" one of his attendants sycophantically added.

"Silence!" the Caliph commanded over the court's whispers.  "You would have done better to kill me last night, thief, and not suffer my wrath," the Caliph threatened, his distrustful eyes locked on Sinbad.

Sinbad tried to answer the serious accusation.

"I would never dream of doing you harm, my Caliph.  I know nothing of what has passed with the night.  I was in my bedchambers with two of my wives.  My third wife was in the adjoining room.  Any of them can tell you I was home all the while..."

Kharim Ahmadi interrupted.   "What else would they say?  They're your wives; their statements cannot be trusted. They may fear reprisals at home," the vizier proffered, adding the last bit as insult.

Another round of gasps rose from the court.

Sinbad could not keep quiet in the face of these vile accusations made by a man he knew to be of such low character.

"You bastard son of a dog! I smell your hand in this! You and that wicked whore daughter of yours!" he spat at the lessor vizier.

"What is to be done with the criminal?" the Caliph regally inquired of the court over their hushed conferring.

Lessor Vizier Kharim Ahmadi answered.

"The law is clear: a thief caught stealing in the bazaar will lose his hand, but to be caught stealing from the Caliph, well...one must pay with their head," he announced as the gallery again gasped. "It is the law," he arrogantly adjudicated.

Again, Sinbad could not hold his tongue with such pronouncements flying.

"It will be *you* that is beheaded—for *your* treachery against the Caliph!" he yelled at the vizier.

As the throne room buzzed with the court's deliberations, the captain of the Palace Guard entered the chamber and approached the Caliph. He bent down and whispered into the monarch's ear.

The guard related that the ongoing search of the palace, initiated after the night's nefarious events, had turned up no one not permitted on the grounds. However, the Caliph's twelve-year-old daughter, Princess Aaliyah (one of the Caliph's seventeen daughters), was missing, nowhere to be found.

The soldier passed some object to the Caliph, and whatever news it carried, it was obvious to all in the court that the Caliph was even more shocked than he had been.

"It is one thing for you to attack me and thieve my treasures, but for you to steal my own blood!" the Caliph yelled as he held out his hand, dangling from which was a distinctive pendant of worked gold and ruby, holding a tiger's claw.

All in Baghdad knew of the pendant, and the story of

Sinbad's voyage during which he slew the beast and cut off its claw. He often wore the treasure on special occasions, so all in the court knew its owner. But Sinbad hadn't seen the necklace in weeks, and he had imagined it to be lost amongst the heaps and chests of treasure littering his mansion, as other trinkets had been misplaced before.

"The Claw! How did you come by it, my Caliph?" Sinbad confusedly inquired.

Ignoring Sinbad's question, the Caliph continued with sobbing anger:

"I treated you as a son, and this is how you repay me! Betrayal!" the Caliph angrily exclaimed. In his mind, Sinbad was obviously also involved in the disappearance of his precious daughter.

"Take him to the dungeon!" the Caliph ordered the guards. Speaking as if Sinbad was already absent, the furious monarch continued, "He is to be beheaded at sundown tomorrow. And, if he gives no word of my daughter by that time, his family will suffer his fate as well."

Still reeling from his sudden and unbelievable reversal of fortune, Sinbad was led to the dungeon and unceremoniously thrown into a cell. As the heavy iron-bar door clanked shut, he began to take notice of his dank, dreary surroundings, and a startling sight met his gaze. Occupying the adjacent cell was a giant of a man. Although he was sitting on the floor with his back against the wall and his knees pulled up to his massive chest, Sinbad could still see that this was a man of unusually large stature. Beyond his exceptional size, the man also stood out due to his elaborately inked skin. Even in the dimly lit dungeon, Sinbad could see that almost every visible patch of his skin was covered in intricate tattoos, including his face. The patterns of lines and dots swirled and eddied up and down his arms and legs, accentuating the lines of his physical attributes and, along with his powerfully muscled frame, gave the man a fearsome appearance akin to that of some far-away island savage. On one of his voyages, Sinbad had seen similar tattoos worn by men who inhabited islands in the far eastern seas, but none as elaborate as this man's.

The strange man took notice of Sinbad's inspection, and he stood and stretched like a waking cat without a care. He wore a simple tunic that hung down to mid-thigh, the plain fabric gathered at the waist with a belt. As he shook out of his face thick, wavy black hair that fell to his shoulders, the man set his intense dark eyes upon Sinbad.

"Me called Fetu. Who you be?" the giant asked amiably in a low, rumbling voice.

"My name is Sinbad," he answered, even more impressed with the man's size now that he was standing.

"Uh! Nooooo!? Sinbad? Sailor Sinbad, captain man?" Fetu mused in disbelief.

"Aye, but now only captain of a jail cell," Sinbad lamented, gesturing to the locked door.

"Why you be here?" the giant asked.

"There is treachery afoot in Baghdad, in the royal court. The Caliph is in danger. There's been a...misunderstanding." Sinbad ended his explanation, again baffled by his predicament.

"Ah," Fetu acknowledged. He then asked a question that was obviously one he had mulled over for some time.

"The stories Fetu hear, about you voyages, can they be true?" he inquired.

Sinbad chuckled.

"Well, what have you heard?"

"Fetu have heard there be things more wilder than dreams." His eyes opened wide. "Big mana, good and bad. These things make Fetu think: Fetu, if ever in Baghdad, hope to find this sailor man called Sinbad, hear stories for self," he excitedly explained.

Fetu's demeanor became contemplative.

"Finally here Baghdad...but everything Fetu do—they say 'not permitted.' Fetu end up in bars." He opened his eyes wide and stuck out his tongue in a ritualistic display as he barked and shook the cell door.

He smiled broadly for a moment, then got serious again

and furrowed his brow.

"Fetu sad locked, many days now, no way to find this 'Sinbad' man...but find you here!" He burst with exuberance. "This good mana, Captain!"

Sinbad smiled back.

"How did you hear of my name?" Sinbad was curious how this wanderer from far away could have heard of him.

"When Fetu sail far, far from home, sail with island man, with black man, with white man, start to hear stories. Fetu cannot believe them!"

Sinbad attested, "As sure as I am standing here this day, the stories are true."

"Ah!" Fetu's eyes were wide with wonder. He continued trying to satiate his burning curiosity.

"But, it be said Captain Sinbad only live on land now, never again on seas. No voyages more."

"It is true." Sinbad nodded. "Until this morning, my life was good, as good as a man could hope, so I've let many opportunities for adventure pass."

Sinbad leaned against the stone wall and let his back slide down until he was sitting on the floor. He somberly continued, with Fetu listening intently on the other side of the iron bars.

"But I never dreamed that life off the sea would find me here." He stared off into the dungeon darkness.

Fetu slid down the wall and sat next to Sinbad.

The two men sat in silence while the time passed. As Sinbad's mind raced through the events of the previous night, he was sure Kharim Ahmadi and his daughter were responsible for the attack on the Caliph and the kidnapping of the princess. But what he could do to catch the criminals and clear his name eluded him. Fetu seemed content with just sitting next to the legendary captain.

After a short while in the silence, Sinbad was startled by the sudden sounds of lock mechanisms clicking, and the stealthy footfalls of sandaled feet moving down the dungeon corridor. Then, in a whisper, a familiar voice issued forth from the darkness.

"Captain? Captain Sinbad, where are you?"

A man's face peered into Sinbad's cell. His hawk-like face, accented by narrow, shifty eyes and a scruffy beard, affected the countenance of a street ruffian.

"Captain! Praise Allah, I found you!" the man exclaimed in hushed excitement.

"Naseem!" Sinbad responded in amazement. "How did you get in here?"

"There is a reason they call me the Thief of Baghdad," the man answered with a devious grin. "I've escaped from this dungeon a dozen times. I even have my own set of keys." He jingled the ring, and his grin widened.

"Good man, Naseem!" Sinbad responded.

The Thief tried several keys until he found the one to unlock Sinbad's cell.

"Do the same favor for my friend here," Sinbad asked, gesturing to Fetu's cell door.

"Aye, Captain. A friend of yours is a friend of m..."

Naseem's voice trailed off, and he instinctively recoiled as he took his first notice of the tattooed giant.

Fetu smiled broadly, his white teeth gleaming in the dungeon darkness.

A moment later, Sinbad and Fetu were free, and the three men moved cautiously down the dimly lit tunnel.

"I know of a secret exit at the far end of this corridor," Naseem explained as he led them.

Just outside the cells, a dungeon guard lay dead on the stone floor, the slit in his throat dripping into the growing crimson pool beneath him. Sinbad hadn't even heard a scuffle. He knew this was some of the silent, deadly work of the Thief.

"Free these other prisoners," Sinbad suggested. "The commotion of their escape will distract the palace guards."

Naseem nodded and complied.

The motley collection of cutthroats, thieves, and beggars rushed out of their unlocked cells and scurried down the corridor toward the main entrance to the dungeon, in the opposite direction to Naseem's secret exit.

As Sinbad and his companions reached the seemingly dead end of the corridor, they could here frantic yells and the sounds of fighting coming from far down the tunnel. The freed prisoners had obviously reached the main guard post, and a pitched battle between the criminals and the palace sentries had begun.

Naseem's skilled hands moved up and down the stone blocks in one corner of the corridor's termination and one of the stones slid back and over, revealing a narrow tunnel at the end of which was a distant sliver of daylight.

The three men slipped into the secret passageway, and Naseem slid back the stone, closing the entrance behind them. Squatting down and pulling in his massive chest, Fetu was barely able to squeeze his giant frame through the low, constricted passage.

They traversed the tunnel and emerged behind one of the pillars of the outer palace wall. They came out into the bright light of morning where the hectic bustle of the Great Bazaar of Baghdad spread out before them in all its astounding sights and sounds and smells. The chaotic mix of merchants and hagglers traded wares from around the world, and so exotic was the throng that, with minimal disguise, even Fetu could move about without attracting much attention.

Using his deft trade craft, Naseem pilfered several scarves and a cloak that would aid Sinbad and Fetu in concealing their identities. Sinbad wrapped a scarf about his head in a turban, and Fetu covered his conspicuous inked skin with the cloak hanging over his shoulders and a swath of fabric around his head and covering his face.

Even outside the palace walls, they could still hear the confusion caused by the other escaped prisoners, and in this moment of relative safety, Naseem imparted what he knew about the nefarious events of the previous night.

"One of my palace spies tells me it was Zahra who was behind the theft of the Caliph's ring and the abduction of the princess. Aided by her magician master, she has taken both and fled to Basrah where her ship waits. She has her vizier father wrapped around her finger, doing her bidding. He seeks your demise so he can solely influence the Caliph."

"I thought as much, the treacherous dogs!" Sinbad cursed. "This 'master,'" he queried, "what is his name; where can he be found?"

"None know. 'The Master' is the only name I've heard. Master of what, or who bestowed upon him the title, none can say. They *do* say he lives on an island somewhere in the southern Arabian Sea," Naseem reported.

Sinbad contemplated the situation for a moment and then issued his orders to Naseem.

"Take a fast horse and ride to Basrah as quickly as you can. Find Ali. Tell him to gather the crew and ready my ship to sail. See what word you can hear on the docks about Zahra's destination. Watch her ship. I'll fall in with a camel caravan traveling the Royal Road to Basrah. I'll meet you there before the sun rises twice."

"But, Captain, I have no fast horse," Naseem regretfully explained with a shrug.

"Now, that wouldn't stop a man possessing your certain set of skills, would it?" Sinbad asked seriously.

Naseem flashed his wide, devious grin.

"See you in Basrah," he replied before disappearing into the crowded bazaar.

Sinbad turned to Fetu.

"Well, my friend, you're free. What will you do now?" he asked of the giant.

"If Captain Sinbad be headed out to sea, Fetu would follow. It why Fetu in Baghdad," he explained, again exhibiting his quick exuberance.

"Very well. Let's find a caravan to join," Sinbad said with a smile as he gave Fetu a comradely pat on his tall shoulder.

Sinbad knew he couldn't go back to his mansion as the palace guards were surely watching, perhaps even there holding his family hostage, awaiting an unthinkable fate. So he went to see a merchant in the bazaar, an old family friend, who loaned him some traveling supplies and two camels.

By mid-day, Sinbad and Fetu were on the backs of their

marching camels in a long line with another hundred more dromedaries, all on their way to Basrah. With scarves covering their faces in the eternally blowing sand, and with the wide variety of travelers in the train, the fugitives appeared to be nothing more than another two merchants heading for the main port city.

At sunset, the caravan stopped for the night and a tent city sprang up in the desert.

After pitching their tent, Sinbad and Fetu shared a light meal of dried meat and dates before settling down for some welcome rest after the hectic events of the previous day.

But outside their tent, diabolical happenings were unfolding. Just after midnight, a wisp of swirling mist twirled down out of the night sky, and in the moon-cast shadows of a thorn bush, the Master's vaporous imp materialized, its small, leering face peering out from the lines of broken shade.

Again, the little devil suddenly held a small fife in the claws of one of its airy hands. But this time, when the thing brought the evil instrument to its lips, no mere illusion of disguise was the result. The unhearable music of the pipe summoned another servant of evil.

Up out of the nighted desert sands writhed an abominable horror from the ancient nightmares of men. A colossal cobra, obsidian-black and with a head as big as that of a pony, emerged from its place of slumber in terrible old memories, called back into this world to do the Master's dark bidding. The scales on its curling body glistened in the moonlight as the monster silently slithered out of the shadows and toward Sinbad's tent. The imp watched intently from its hiding place behind the thorns, and a sinister grin cracked its tiny gargoyle countenance.

The monstrous serpent floated noiselessly across the sands, its undulating body side-winding to the tent's door. Its probing forked tongue flicked frantically as its head pushed aside the door flap, and its icy yellow eyes peered inside, searching for those whom the Master marked for doom.

The silent intruder's movements hadn't awakened the tent's occupants, but its parting of the tent's door had let in the slight cool desert breeze. The monster slithered into the tent, and when at Sinbad's feet, its head reared up off the rug and its hood flared wide. It exposed massive, dripping fangs that glistened in the faint light, and the monster prepared to strike.

Just at that moment, the night breeze roused Sinbad, and he woke to see the swaying silhouette of the giant serpent framed in the parted door. For a split-second, his waking mind couldn't decide if he was still asleep, but luckily, it was just an instant of indecision.

Sinbad rolled across the rug just as the snake struck, and its head came down on the bare carpet.

"Fetu!" Sinbad yelled, and the giant jumped up, his eyes wide as he took in the shocking sight of the monster snake.

"Captain!" Fetu's yell was a burst of concern.

Fetu grabbed the body of the serpent, as big around as his thigh, and pulled it away from Sinbad as the cobra struck a second time. The snake's head again plowed into the rug, and Sinbad pulled up the corner of the carpet and flipped it up and over the monster's head. Fetu continued to wrestle with the snake's powerful black coils as Sinbad grabbed his dagger and plunged it hilt-deep through the rug and into the back of the snake's neck. The giant ophidian's agitated movements ripped the dagger's blade back and forth through the snake's flesh, and in a moment it fell still.

Both men were breathing heavily, and still gripping the snake's lifeless body as a bizarre transformation occurred. The long, black form of the snake burst into a line of thick smoke that sifted through their fingers before rolling into the air and out of the tent.

Sinbad and Fetu rushed out of the tent after the misty form and saw it twist up into the dark night sky.

"Look there, Captain!" Fetu pointed to the Master's tiny servant hiding behind the thorn bush.

Both men watched as the imp also lost solid form and became a wisp of mist that darted up into the night and out of sight.

In response to the commotion, other travelers began emerging from nearby tents but there was nothing left for them to see apart from the two bewildered men.

"Let's gather the camels. We'll leave for Basrah at once," Sinbad somberly announced.

"Aye, Captain. This bad mana. Fetu no like this place."

They rode through the moonlit night unmolested, and by mid-morning they had reached the outskirts of Basrah.

After finding Naseem, Sinbad learned that the Royal Army had troops guarding the port, and all departing vessels were being searched. To avoid any royal entanglements, Ali, Sinbad's first mate, sailed the ship down the coast a short distance where it was still waiting for its captain.

Naseem also told what he knew of Zahra's ship and its destination. Just after midnight, her ship had sailed out of Basrah, headed due south toward the open ocean of the southern Arabian Sea. Zahra's ship had only been able to evade the royal troops after a strange mist appeared out of the clear night sky, harassing and distracting the soldiers just long enough for the wicked woman to leave with the ring and the kidnapped princess.

The three men left immediately to rendezvous with Sinbad's waiting ship.

By mid-day they had reached the ship, which was teeming with sailors going about the duties of preparing the vessel for a voyage. Sinbad stepped onto the deck, and a cheer went up from the loyal crew.

"Good work, Ali!" Sinbad praised his right-hand man. "How long before we can get under way?" the captain inquired.

"Just give the word, Captain. She's ready to sail," Ali proudly replied.

"Cast off! Man the oars! When she's clear of the harbor, set sail for the open ocean!" Sinbad barked the orders all the men, including Fetu, yearned to hear. With their minds swimming in thoughts of adventure, the sailors swarmed across the deck like excited ants.

Sinbad inspected the crew.

"Ah, Faraz...and Rahim—what would a voyage be without you two? Good to see you among the crew. To the rest of you—it's certain you've heard the tales, and you know we sail into danger, but remember this: the stories couldn't be told if ship and crew never returned!" The men cheered. "Our voyage *will* be perilous, but our courage is needed by the Caliph...all of Arabia needs your stout hearts." A look of stern determination came over Sinbad's face as he continued. "We sail in search of a magician - not to ask for the aid of his powers but to deliver the final justice owed him for his evil deeds. We will suffer his black treachery, no doubt, but I am confident we will prevail. We must." Sinbad's mood lightened a bit and a slight smile cracked his face. "And when we do prevail, if the magician possesses anything of value...well, then it will be ours." Hearty hoots and howls rang from the crew as Sinbad proceeded. "And this I promise you—every man, woman and child in all of the Empire shall know your names upon our return!"

Another round of boisterous cheers rose from the sea dogs.

Once out at sea, Sinbad felt a wave of relaxing familiarity wash over him. A bright summer sun shone down onto the infinite ocean, and the sweet smell of the sea filled his nostrils. Crewmen scurried about the decks, and the breezes murmured with the thrum of cordage and the lap of waves. With the wind in his hair, and his hands on the ship's wheel, Sinbad felt at home again.

Zahra had at least a half day's lead on them, but Sinbad knew his ship to be faster under its full-bellied sails, and he hoped to catch up to her in a day or two.

At the end of their second day on the ocean, just as the sun set, a lookout called down the sighting of sails far off on the southern horizon, and Sinbad eased the wheel to intercept the ship he was sure belonged to Zahra.

As Zahra's ship drew closer across the calm, moonlit seas, Sinbad's crew prepared for battle.

But when Sinbad's ship chased to within a bow's shot,

Zahra's ship made an unexpected maneuver, tacking straight into the wind, greatly reducing the vessel's speed. Sinbad turned his ship in behind it.

By the time Sinbad realized it was a trap, it was too late. From Zahra's ship began to pour a great cloud of mist. So much of the stuff billowed out behind the vessel that a bank of the fog started to form, drifting toward Sinbad's ship. The cloud was so large that, even with heavy evasive maneuvers, Sinbad couldn't avoid the mist, and it began to envelop his ship.

The green gas choked the crew, and men began falling to the deck. After a few moments, all aboard the vessel had been put to sleep by the foul fog.

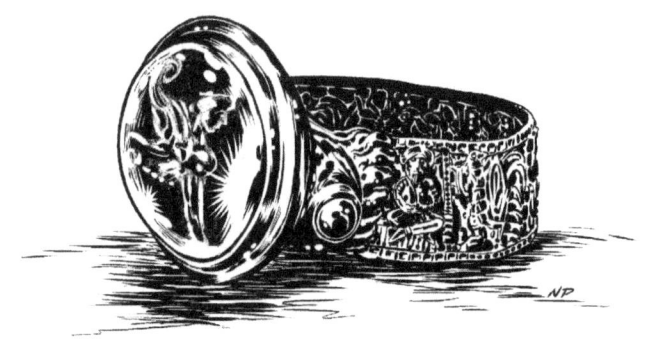

Just as the sun peeked over the morning horizon, Zahra's ship arrived at the Master's island. At a derelict dock where half a dozen other ships in various states of disrepair rose and fell gently with the swells, Zahra and her crew were met by servants of the Master. These were men, but under some powerful spell. Their pale skin, stretched over gaunt frames, was pocked with festering boils and oozing wounds as if injuries suffered long ago hadn't even begun to heal. They had obviously once been sailors, perhaps the very ones that had manned the other vessels, but they would never again feel the freedom of the open ocean. They were irretrievably ensorcelled. Even the murderess Zahra recoiled at the sight of the living dead men.

"Bring to Master..." one rotting man slowly hissed.

Three of the entranced men led Zahra and the princess away while another ten stayed at the dock. When Zahra was out of sight, the Master's servants attacked her crew. Those that survived were taken to await the same fate that had befallen the servants.

Zahra was surprised by her own nervousness. Just this instant, she was beginning to realize that her thoughts and actions had not been her own, that she was also under some kind of spell. She thought of the mesmerized men, and how they obviously suffered some dark influence. The momentary feeling of doubt passed, but it was still unsettling, even to one as cold as she. Zahra tightly gripped the ring on her finger.

The confused and afraid little princess, still groggy from Zahra's drugging, commanded enough of her senses to realize this was an evil, dangerous place, and she tried to run into the jungle. But one of the men grabbed her, and pulled her along by the arm.

The servants led them through the jungle down a wide, stone-paved path to a large clearing where two more servants waited on an expansive marble platform. As they climbed the few steps up to the low stage, one of the waiting servants kicked the roll of a wide rug, and the carpet unfurled to lie flat on the marble. The men bade Zahra and the terrified princess sit at the center of the intricately woven carpet, and two of the servants joined them. Another demonstration of the Master's power was about to commence.

The edges of the green silk carpet sparkled and shimmered, and the gold-tassel fringe began to flutter in waves that darted down its lengths. A colony of giant black bats flew from the jungle trees and circled above, shading the magic carpet from the light of the morning sun. The carpet and its riders were lifted off the marble and rose straight up into the air. The princess grabbed onto Zahra's arm as they flew through the morning mist high over the island's rocky terraces toward the eerie crimson castle that loomed above.

"Where are they taking us?" the girl asked. "I want to see my father!" she imperiously demanded.

"Hush, child," Zahra chided. "The Caliph holds no sway on this island. He cannot find you here. Feel honored, girl. We go to meet your new master." The young princess didn't understand, but kept her tongue silent. Zahra again clutched at the Caliph's ring.

The carpet slowly set down on another marble stage near the tall castle wall, and the shading bats dispersed, disappearing back into the jungle trees far below. Though it was a bright, early morning, the sky around the castle was now darkened as if it were evening.

Inside the wall, through massive, iron-bound teak gates, the giant conical structure rose in half a dozen shrinking tiers to the tall central tower. Seemingly carved from a mountain of deep red rock, the castle was surrounded by a moat of impassible darkness, where it looked as though the world dropped away into an endless night. A bridge of air and sea came up out of the abyss, and the group passed over the moat and entered the Master's citadel.

The servants led the two women through the grand halls of the dark palace, where strange titterings and demonic howls moved with darting silhouettes in the shadows. Dreadful stone figures lined the chambers, and a sickeningly sweet smell wafted from burning braziers.

Lit only by the false evening light of the morning, the rays of altered sunlight cut the shadows through tall, narrow slits split in the crimson stone walls, and marked the path through the castle into the chambers of the Master. In a tall, round antechamber, at the center of which was an altar of dark stone and ivory, he waited.

Upon first sight of the Master, Zahra was struck by his terrible magnificence. His radiant eyes, set against his dark skin, stood out in the darkened chamber, and seemed to be two glowing orbs floating above his shimmering black-and-gold silk robes.

Despite her trepidation, Zahra rushed up to the sorcerer and knelt before him.

"I have done as you commanded, my Master," she offered in obedience.

"Yes. I see she of the al-Rashid bloodline has come to stay as my guest," he slowly hissed with his radiant eyes fixed on the little princess. The Master seemed to ignore Zahra's presence. "My dear little one, welcome to your new home," he said to the princess with an unctuous tone. The Master approached the girl and, with her face riddled with fear, she tried to back away, but was blocked by the servants. "You must be tired after your long journey," the Master continued, with his insincere affection. His words were dripping with malevolence. "Let me help you sleep," he whispered as he waved his hand.

The princess began to go limp, but she was taken up by the servants before she fell to the floor. They laid her on the altar, and the Master spread his arms out over her, the wide sleeves of his black silk robes unfurled like devil's wings. He voiced an incantation in some unknown ancient language, and with another wave of his hand, an ill spell was cast. A cocoon of pulsing magic wrapped over the princess, and a shocking necromantic transformation began. Her form was undergoing some kind of unholy alteration. To Zahra, it seemed the little girl was aging rapidly under the shimmering cloak of wizardry.

Zahra crawled up behind the Master and reached out to caress his thigh. The visits from the imp had horribly altered her mind, and it was obvious she harbored a lecherous craving for the sorcerer's affections. Zahra shuddered with pleasure as she touched him.

The Master wheeled, and with a wave of his hand, some unseen force pushed Zahra back, much to her surprise. She fell back onto the stone floor, and another wave of uncertain fear washed through her mind. But the hesitation again passed, and she seemed undeterred from her desires.

"What plans have you made for Arabia, my Master?" she inquired, ignoring his rebuff. "My father and I wish to serve you in any ways we can."

"Soon, I will take the princess as my bride, and the marriage shall be consummated," the Master announced. "She will be mother to the new ruler of the Caliphate. Born of the royal al-Rashid bloodline and schooled in the dark arts, my son, in time, will hold dominion over the world!"

With this revelation, Zahra burned with jealousy. The heavy bewitching inflicted upon her by the imp had given her a possessive, erotic lust for the Master. The idea that another woman should be with him, and a child at that, made Zahra plead.

"It was my greatest hope that I might be bestowed with

such an honor, exalted one."

The Master laughed maniacally.

"You?! With your gutter blood?!" he sneered at her. "Your father is the bastard son of a thousand desert dogs, you filth! I wouldn't even let you suckle the child if we were lost in the desert!" Again he laughed contemptuously.

Shaken, but still determined, she tried to reason with the wizard who stood towering over her.

"The princess is but a child, infertile, unable yet to bear young. Can I not serve that purpose for you, my Master?"

Again the Master jeered, his laugh thick with menace.

"Ha! You foul, ignorant creature...and now you want me to mount you." He shook his head in condescending disbelief. Then a deadly serious look came over the sorcerer. "You have served your purpose!" He again outstretched his arms, and focused his eerie eyes on Zahra. "I know you have disobeyed my commands, peon, and used the magic for your own trifling purposes." His face contorted into a countenance of pure evil. "Did you think I would not know? The servant of the Ebon Globe sees all...and tells all!" His voice echoed ominously through the chamber.

Again Zahra's strong character suddenly pushed through the spell that clouded her mind, and once more she realized the extreme danger she was in. In hopes of defense, she raised her hand with the Star of Percepolis glittering on one finger, but immeasurable fear was still written across her face.

"I care not the least of your new trinket, petty thief," the Master said dismissively. "But had you not returned with the girl..." Without expressing it, he let Zahra contemplate the wrath that would have befallen her. "Did you truly believe the Caliph's worthless charm would protect you? Countless stones in this chamber alone are worth more and possess more powerful magic...magic beyond your wildest dreams." He gestured to ancient treasures and relics that crowded the stone ledges ringing the room. "In truth, I sense no magic at all within your precious costume jewelry."

And the sorcerer was correct in his determination. The

magic of the Star could only be called by wearers pure of heart and deed, of which Zahra was neither. On her finger, it was nothing more than a ring.

The Master extended a hand toward Zahra, and she felt a great weight pressing in upon her from all sides. She screeched in agony as the pressure began to burn like hellfire, and she cowered behind her raised hand that wore the inert gem. Zahra crawled backwards into a shallow alcove, trying to flee her fate, but it was to no avail. Shimmering rings of necromantic death flowed from the Master's hand and encircled her, immolating under the powerful constriction, and transmogrifying Zahra into a shriveling corpse. It took but a moment for life to be squeezed and burned completely out of her, and Zahra's desiccated body crumpled to the floor in a bony pile of dust within her unburned robes, the Star still glimmering on one of her broken, skeletal fingers.

At about the time Zahra's ship arrived at the Master's island, Sinbad and his crew began to awaken from the restless slumber induced by the foul green fog.

"Damn my fool's eagerness!" Sinbad chastised himself. "She tricked us into a trap," he lamented as the other men began to stir.

It was now sunrise, hours after they had succumbed to the mist, and the poisonous air had long since dissipated. In the early day light, Sinbad and the revived crewmen fed themselves and took stock of the ship. She'd suffered no damage and nothing was found to be missing. With a quick sighting of the sun's position and a reading of the astrolabe, Sinbad determined that the ship hadn't drifted far from where they had encountered Zahra's vessel.

They set sail south, hoping to again catch up with the ship. Sinbad was unwaveringly determined to rescue the princess. With little thought of the need to clear his name by retrieving the Star, Sinbad was now focused on saving the innocent little girl. There was some reason she had been kidnapped alive, so he was sure there was still time to find her unharmed.

Around the bright mid-day, a strange call came down from the lookout.

"Ship! Dead ahead! Ablaze in bright gold fire! Closing fast!" the man yelled down in halting disbelief.

"Gold fire?!" Sinbad called back as he grabbed his spyglass and ran toward the bow of the ship.

There was a moment of silence after the captain's call and the first mate cracked his whip.

"Come back, lookout! Captain's call!" Ali yelled upward.

"Aye, Captain! Gold flame! It looks like...it's as if...I don't know what it is, Captain, but it's bearing down fast!" the baffled man yelled.

Through his spyglass, Sinbad saw what at first looked like a tiny flicker of gold light far off on the horizon. A moment later the light was larger, and as the lookout had said, it shimmered like a spot of golden fire where the deep jade sea met the infinite blue sky.

As the object drew nearer, Sinbad could see that it wasn't aflame, but instead highly reflective in the bright sunlight, as if it were made of some shining metal such as gold.

Eventually, it became evident the thing was indeed some kind of vessel, seemingly constructed of lustrous golden metal, but part of the reason it looked aflame and flickering in the far distance was that as the object moved through the water, it had a curious side-to-side motion, as if were...swimming.

As it closed in, Sinbad could see the golden ship had some kind of spar standing up from its low deck.

Sinbad maneuvered his ship out of an intersecting course, and the strange vessel corrected its course to intercept. It was definitely coming toward them.

"It's a giant gold fish, Captain! As big as a whale! A great golden marlin, she is!" the lookout yelled down in amazement.

The strange, shimmering object continued bearing down on his ship, and as it drew closer, Sinbad could see no sails or oars propelling the vessel. It did indeed seem to be swimming along the ocean's surface like a fish.

The giant gold fish had been moving at an even clip with regular motions, until suddenly, with several quick, powerful strokes of its tail, the oddity rose up in the water before nosing down, and the gold gleam of its tall dorsal fin disappeared into the sea.

"Can you see it?!" Sinbad yelled up to the lookout.

"Nay, Captain! She's gone!" the lookout called back.

As Sinbad and the crew scanned the sea around their vessel, none could see any trace of the marlin until the lookout spotted the fish still speeding toward them.

"Dead ahead! Just below the surface and coming in fast!" he yelled down frantically.

With a bursting of the sea's surface that sent a huge spray of water into the air, the Golden Marlin breached like its non-metallic namesake with its long gold bill pointing toward the sky. In the instant the fish's body was visible, Sinbad could definitely see that the thing was not some monstrous gold mutation of nature, but in fact some manner of giant machine. After its powerful tail strokes lifted nearly all of its impressive body out of the ocean, the thing splashed down in front of Sinbad's vessel, creating a huge wave that violently rocked the ship, throwing crewmen from their feet and sending them to the deck.

The sea calmed and then again all was quiet. The Golden Marlin was nowhere to be seen.

The men pulled themselves to their feet, and again spied the waves for a sight of the thing.

"It's coming up from below!" Ali yelled a warning.

Sinbad looked over the gunnel and saw a flickering glint of gold flying up through the water beneath the ship.

"Brace yourselves!" the captain ordered just before the impact.

There was a tremendous collision accompanied by the

thunderous sounds of cracking timber. The ship was violently jarred by the impact, and the Marlin's massive gold spear burst up through the deck, impaling an unlucky crewman.

The bottom of the hull was cracked open like an eggshell, and water began flooding into the lower deck of the ship, causing the vessel to list to one side.

The giant metal marlin sank back down into the water and its gold gleam disappeared into the depths. A few moments later, it surfaced some distance from the ship and again the strange machine swam toward Sinbad's vessel at a tremendous pace. The Golden Marlin was set on another collision course.

The instant before the monstrous machine again violently crashed into the hull, Fetu yelled a tribal call and made an astounding leap from the sinking vessel into the water alongside the metallic fish.

Again the vessels violently collided, and the mechanical monster's dorsal fin cut deep into the side of the ship's hull, sending sea water pouring into all of its compartments.

With this brutal jolt, Sinbad was thrown from the stern into the water, and he watched his broken vessel quake as the giant fish pulled itself from the wreckage of what had been his ship. Whomever piloted this marauding machine, they would pay, Sinbad promised himself as he swam toward the Golden Marlin.

Sinbad's ship began breaking apart, and after a few moments, all that was left floating in the water was debris and the surviving crewmen.

As the sailors clung to the floating pieces of their shattered ship, the gold machine, now seemingly idle, kept station on the water's surface a short distance upwind. As he swam toward it, Sinbad heard a metallic clank and saw Fetu, who was now standing on the fish, jump back from its head. A shuttered vent on the forehead of the Marlin opened and a yellow-green mist began spraying forth. It created a low cloud that hung over the wreckage, covering the crewmen treading water.

"Look there!  Again, the green mist of sleep!" Ali warned the crew as the cloud began rolling over them.

Sinbad and Fetu were the only ones out of reach of the stretching veil of green sleep.  The two men had to watch helplessly as the crew was again afflicted by the poison gas.

Fetu continued investigating the strange contraption and could see several small round windows in the gold skin of the fish.  Inside the object, he spied the vague outlines of figures moving about.

"Captain, there be men inside!" Fetu yelled to Sinbad, who had nearly reached the Marlin by this time.

"Get the dogs out!" the Captain ordered as he swam.

"Aye!" the giant answered.

There appeared to be two entrances into the fish, with the larger main hatch on the forehead and a smaller hatch halfway down the tail.  Fetu crawled along the machine to the aft hatch and squatted down on top of it.  The massive muscles in his legs and down his back flexed, and he fixed his wide-eyed gaze on the hatch's handle.  His huge hands gripped the bar, and he again contorted his face into a fierce tribal display with his tongue out.  With a terrifying yell, he lifted his head, and his muscles rippled and knotted under his dark, inked skin as he pulled with all his considerable might.  The locking bar creaked and groaned under the great stress, and eventually, with a loud crack, it gave way, sending Fetu staggering backward, trying to balance on the tail of the fish.

By this time, Sinbad had reached the Marlin and climbed aboard.

Fetu leaned forward and pulled up the hatch.  A waft of a vile stench akin to rotting flesh burst up out of the portal, and the dead, blood-shot eyes of one of the occupants stared out.

Fetu flashed his tribal glare, accompanied by a loud bark.

After remaining still for a moment, the only response from the seemingly entranced man was a slow, hostile moan.

"Huh?!" Fetu exclaimed.  In all the years of his travels, never once had his war face failed to elicit some noticeable reaction.

After the moment of surprise, Fetu was jolted back to the present as the hissing man thrust a knife up at him. The giant's fist came down like a hammer, knocking the man unconscious. Fetu grabbed him before he fell, and pulled him up through the hatch, tossing him into the water like a rag doll.

"Crazy man!" Fetu warned Sinbad, who had seen the entire incident.

Sinbad pushed his scimitar into Fetu's hands, believing the blade would be difficult to wield in the narrow confines of the mechanical fish. With some idea of what he might meet after seeing Fetu's altercation with the first strange occupant, Sinbad ignored the narrow ladder and jumped straight down into the hatch. He drew his dagger as he fell, and when he hit the deck below, he could see another man staggering toward him. The man swung a curved dagger at him, but Sinbad jumped aside and grabbed the man's knife arm at the wrist. Sinbad twisted the man's arm down and plunged the man's own blade into his gut. But this normally fatal injury only slightly weakened the man, and he continued to struggle in Sinbad's grasp. It wasn't until Sinbad stabbed his dagger straight up under the man's chin and into his brain that the entranced man ceased attacking. The man crumpled to the floor, and with heavy breaths, Sinbad took in his first look at the inside of the mechanical wonder.

The giant fish was some kind of fantastic mechanism constructed in form to resemble and even swim like a real marlin, only much larger and gleaming gold from the tip of its bill to the end of its tail. With its long gold spear, the unbelievable vessel was nearly as long as Sinbad's ship, while on the inside she was no wider than a camel is long.

Fetu had followed Sinbad down into the fish, and he looked with wary wonder upon the insides of the Golden Marlin.

"This be slave ship, Captain!" Fetu asserted with concern.

Sinbad also noticed the rows of shallow, seat-like

conforms along either side of the inner hull, ten in all, each position fitted with strong leathern restraints. The two entranced men who had been in the strange vessel were obviously on a mission to incapacitate seamen with the sleeping mist, and then kidnap them to be doomed to a dead life as servants for the Master.

After this troubling revelation gave him pause for a moment, Sinbad continued inspecting the inside of the mechanical wonder. Its tail section, about two-thirds its length, was constructed of nested, telescoping segments that perfectly fit into one another, allowing the machine to bend and swim like a fish. By some magic, water was kept from seeping into the vessel between the segments. A collection of copper tubes ran the length of the Golden Marlin both beneath the grated deck and along the ceiling, animating the machinery with some kind of magical hydraulic power. All the tubes ran to a giant mechanical heart that was suspended on gold beams in the middle of the enclosure near the head of the fish.

The golden heart was about the size of a colt's body, and through gaps in its outer shell Sinbad could see gears and other finely-machined parts turning and winding within the necromantic mechanical power plant. Glowing gems set in gold mounts could also be seen amongst the intricate, whirling machinery, and small puffs of steam occasionally sprayed from several tubular vents on its surface as the heart quiescently waited to again propel the vessel.

As Sinbad moved to the front of the vessel, he could see the larger main hatch located on the fish's forehead, as well as the apparatus used to disperse the poison gas. A wide tube leading to the shuttered vent on the front of the fish held a spent gold canister, pierced at one end by a retracted spike. Apparently, the canisters were placed in the tube and breached by the sharp spike, releasing the mist that would only flow out the vent. Several more unpierced gold canisters sat in a nearby rack.

In the head of the fish were two seats for the Master's servants. The seats, with stout shoulder straps to hold the occupants, sat behind a kind of display. It was a flat sandstone slab on which simple symbols were carved. Sinbad could identify no controls for direction, no wheel or rudder stick, and he concluded the vessel was automated and required no action from the occupants to direct its motion.

As Sinbad more closely inspected the stone panel, he saw that the symbols, although seemingly carven, were animated. Of particular note was an hourglass symbol that slowly evolved as if the sand was falling in the glass. The other images were also decipherable, such as a representation of the fish floating on the water's surface, and a dashed line extending from the fish down into the ocean's depths. Sinbad deduced the Golden Marlin was on an automated countdown to dive for a return trip to the Master's island.

As the green fog outside the vessel dissipated, blowing away in the slight breeze, Fetu began swimming to the unconscious crewmen floating in the water. After Sinbad opened the large main hatch, he joined Fetu in the grim rescue effort. Many of the men had already drowned, and only the ones that clung to the shipwreck debris were still alive.

Sinbad and Fetu pulled the living into the Golden Marlin and secured them in the seats with the restraints. Among the rescued were Ali and Naseem, but in total, only seven of Sinbad's crew had survived the ordeal.

It was a risky proposition, but out in the open ocean, Sinbad knew their only chance for survival was in the hope the fish would swim them to the safety of land. Whatever "safety" they might encounter on the island of the Master, it was preferable to being stranded at sea.

After the crewmen were recovered and secured, Sinbad and Fetu continued examining the fish's innards. Slight flames of white witchfire danced down the tubes and about the throbbing gold heart, and jewels, glowing in all the colors of the rainbow, twinkled from their settings in intricate carvings and esoteric symbols that covered the gold panels along the inside of the hull. The astounding metalwork and machinery was of a construction never before seen by Sinbad's worldly eyes.

As the carven hourglass symbol on the display stone completed its animation of sand running out, a chime repeatedly sounded, and the display altered. The hourglass symbol was reset and began to pass sand again, only this time much more quickly, and the dashed line leading down into the ocean from the marlin symbol became solid and began to flash like a line carved in the stone that vanished and reappeared repeatedly.

After securing the main hatch, Sinbad ran to the tail of the fish and pulled the aft hatch shut. Although the hatch closed properly, it could not be locked due to the damage that had occurred when Fetu ripped it open.

"I think it's closed," Sinbad unconvincingly assured Fetu. "We'll get wet if it isn't," he added in understatement.

"Fetu fix," the strongman announced.

He grabbed a part of the broken locking mechanism and bent it over the rim of the portal, cinching the hatch tightly closed.

"Good man!" Sinbad praised. "Let's hope it holds," he added, like a gambler throwing dice.

The Golden Marlin's mechanical heart suddenly took on new life, and began to regularly vent strong bursts of steam as its internal workings spun and wound apace. The enchanted jewels within the heart glowed intensely, dimly lighting the interior. The fish's tail started bending back and forth, its nested segments perfectly sliding past each other, and the vessel began propelling itself through the water at increasing speed.

A final, louder chime sounded and the fish began to submerge.

"May Allah bring us luck," prayed Sinbad.

He and Fetu strapped themselves into the front seats and awaited their fate.

As the fish descended, Sinbad looked over his shoulder and noted that a small but constant stream of sea water was spraying into the vessel from around the damaged aft hatch, but some kind of automatic bilge pump was clearing it from the fish, and little pooled under the deck. The hatch seemed as if it would hold.

Down the Golden Marlin plunged, flying through the water at a tremendous pace. Were it not for the strong shoulder straps, Sinbad and Fetu would have fallen upon the display stone, such was the inclination of the fish.

As the ocean's depths darkened around them, the fish's two large eyes, which were actually strange, transparent windows, began emitting light that illuminated the water ahead of the vessel.

Deeper and deeper they dove, and Sinbad and Fetu watched in bewilderment as astounding sea creatures, wondrous and terrifying, approached the Golden Marlin to inspect the curious, unknown inhabitant of this alien undersea world.

Eventually the bottom of the sea rose up out of the darkness beneath the vessel, and the Marlin sped along the seabed, passing sunken hills and valleys. At one point they passed the stunning spectacle of an active undersea volcano as it built a new island that would someday rise to the surface.

As the vessel flew along the ocean bottom, Sinbad continued monitoring the display panel. A compass symbol carved into the stone pointed south, and Sinbad pondered where the fish might be headed, for he knew these waters well and only open ocean lay ahead.

"Captain, here be knife for Fetu!" the giant exclaimed as he surveyed the surroundings.

Next to the forward seats occupied by Sinbad and Fetu was a small cache of bladed weapons. There were several daggers and swords including one that was similar to the scimitar Sinbad carried, but with a blade that was longer and wider, more akin to the giant swords used by executioners for beheadings. This was the steel that had caught Fetu's eye.

Sinbad looked to the aft of the Marlin to check on his unconscious crewmen, and saw they were all still securely strapped into their positions, their heads gently lolling on their shoulders with the easy motions of the swimming fish.

After several hours traveling across the alien undersea landscape, the quiet, darkened ambiance of the fish's interior suddenly altered. New sounds rang out on top of the subtle monotonous noises of the pumping mechanical heart and the gently clanking machinery of the swimming tail, and Sinbad was shaken out of his catnap by a chime and a sudden change on the display stone. The symbol of the Marlin that sat just above the jagged representation of the passing sea floor now had a long, curved line leading from its bill back up to the ocean surface, and a symbol that looked like an island now appeared at the end of the line.

"An island?" Sinbad mused to himself, knowing these waters well and remembering no land.

The Golden Marlin's bill reared up in the deep water, and the fish began swimming toward the surface. The black ocean lightened with the sun's rays as the Marlin ascended until the fish's majestic, gleaming dorsal fin burst through the water's surface and stood up tall in the bright sea air.

Fetu unbuckled the straps that had held him in his seat, and moved passed the still-sleeping crewmen to the aft of the Marlin. He unbent the bar holding the aft hatch closed, pushed open the portal, and climbed the ladder up to the sunlight.

"Captain! It true! There be island!" Fetu exclaimed.

Sinbad also unstrapped himself and stood, craning his neck to get a look through one of the small round windows along the top of the marlin.

"I've sailed these seas a dozen times. There's no island within a thousand leagues of here," the captain bewilderedly responded.

But there it was, right where it shouldn't be: a mysterious island lay dead ahead of the fish.

The island was made up of recognizable land forms arranged in a decidedly unnatural way. As the marlin approached from the north, the medium-sized island looked to have a sliver of jungle along its northern shore abutted steep, cave-riddled cliffs that rose high to a vast, flat jungle plateau that covered most of the land. Out of this wide field of green, near the western shore, rose a colossal rough stone pillar, atop which perched a wondrous crimson castle with a tall central spire.

Sinbad knew an unfortunate decision had to be made. He had hoped the sleeping mist would wear off by the time they had reached the Master's lair, and the crewmen could at least defend themselves against the Master's servants, but it was not to be; all the crewmen remained soundly unconscious.

If he and Fetu remained aboard the Marlin, they would likely be captured along with the drugged crewmen when the Marlin docked. If the fish was constructed for bringing slaves to the island, certainly more of the mesmerized men awaited its arrival.

Sinbad decided the best course of action would be for he and Fetu to swim from the Golden Marlin as it approached the island, and then try to secret into the castle, not only to rescue the princess, but also to help the captured crewmen. It was a risky plan, but the only one he could formulate that had even the slightest chance of success.

As the mechanical fish drew nearer to the island, it swung wide to approach from the west. Sinbad could clearly see there was some kind of dock at the northern tip of the isle where several vessels were moored, one of which looked to be Zahra's. The view from the west also revealed steep, unclimbable cliffs rising from narrow beaches surrounding the rest of the island.

The Marlin seemed to be heading for the gaping entrance to a huge, half-submerged cave into which the sea flooded. Upon the bluff above the cave was a castle outbuilding, and Sinbad could also see the mouths of other caves lining the beach and honeycombing the cliff face. He surmised that there must be a subterranean dock for the Marlin within the grotto, and perhaps a network of tunnels existed throughout the island rock, through which there might be a way to stealthily enter the palace above. It was worth a try, Sinbad concluded.

Fetu collected the giant, long-hilted scimitar he'd been eyeing as Sinbad made a last check of the unconscious crewmen, saying a prayer on their behalf.

As the Golden Marlin approached the massive, stone-block-lined cave entrance, Fetu returned to the aft hatch and climbed out onto the back of the fish.

As he stared in wonder at the strange isle, Fetu was startled by the sight of what looked to be a small wisp of smoke twirling through the air toward the Marlin. Although the mist didn't take any particular form, Fetu thought he recognized what it was, and he yelled a warning.

"Captain! It be the devil wisp!"

Just as Fetu alerted, the wispy mist twirled down into the Marlin through the aft hatch and swirled about Sinbad's head like a cloud of mosquitoes, before it flew to the sleeping crewmen, seemingly inspecting each as it moved from one to another.

Sinbad bolted for the aft of the fish and flew up the ladder, slamming the hatch closed behind him.

The twirling mist shot to the back of the Marlin and pushed up on the hatch, trying to open it, but Fetu slammed it back down and bent the broken bar back over the portal, locking it shut.

Through the small windows along the fish, Sinbad and Fetu could see the mist darting back and forth, trying to escape, but like a genie trapped in a magic lamp, the mist-thing was securely sealed inside.

Sinbad and Fetu slipped off the tail of the Marlin as the giant mechanical fish, still carrying the grim cargo of their sleeping comrades, swam into the cave mouth and disappeared into the darkness.

As the two men swam toward shore, Sinbad could catch no sight of the ocean bottom. Apparently, the island sat atop sheer underwater cliffs that dropped straight down into the depths around the land and, at least on this side of the island, there were no shallows leading up to the beaches.

The area surrounding the cavern the Marlin swam into was nothing but sheer cliffs with no beach to come ashore.

They'd have to swim south a distance to where the cliffs pulled back and a sliver of beach started to grow. Other large caverns opened onto the beach further down, and if Sinbad's hunch was correct, caves leading into the subterranean dock, and maybe even the palace itself, could be found therein. After the brisk swim through an oddly strong current, Sinbad and Fetu climbed out of the crashing surf onto the short and steep rocky beach.

It was late afternoon by the time Sinbad and Fetu made their way down the beach to where the mouth of a huge cavern gaped a way into the belly of the island. The cave entrance was strewn with the rotting bodies and shells of countless sea creatures, obviously preyed upon by something that had ripped the carcasses to pieces.

With scimitars in hand, the two men cautiously entered the wide tunnel. A well-worn path in the sand, covered in strange tracks, led into a series of rough natural hollows, dimly lit by scant slivers of sunlight that fell through great fissures in the rock above. The floor of the cave was also littered with the bleached and shattered shells of ocean animals, but unlike the clutter of dead at the cave entrance, all these seemed to be the remnants of one kind of unknown creature.

The cave that had narrowed as they left the beach eventually opened up and led into a huge cavern where mineral stalagmites as tall as a man spiked up from the cave floor, pointing toward the dripping stalactites hanging down from the tall cavern ceiling. The sweet-smelling sea air of the outer cave gave way to a foul fishy odor that was thick in the weird space.

In the dim light, Sinbad could see that rimming the wide, roughly circular cavern, dotting the floor between the stalagmites, were boulders of curiously uniform size and shape.

Suddenly, like flowers instantly popping up from the desert sand, pairs of small, glistening orbs began rising up from around the strange, similarly shaped rocks. The spheres were as big as a man's fist, and they rose on narrow, dark stocks about the length of a man's forearm.

Sinbad and Fetu warily froze for a moment at the eerie sight, then both started to slowly back their way out of the cavern.

"Captain, the rocks have eyes," Fetu whispered in amazement.

Sinbad had also noticed the objects' likeness to eyes as the things swiveled about and swayed to and fro on their stocks.

"I don't think they're rocks," Sinbad replied. "We'd best leave this place," he warned.

But as they turned to leave the cavern, they saw the tunnel they had entered through was now crowded with strange creatures coming their way. The things began clicking loudly as they frantically swung their seemingly countless alien appendages in aggressive agitation. From their silhouettes, outlined against the small patch of daylight still visible far down the tunnel, Sinbad couldn't guess at what they were, and it wasn't until he turned back toward the massive cavern that his mind settled on an unbelievable, but inescapable, conclusion. The things were some ungodly perversions of nature akin to crabs, only much larger.

Sinbad was well-acquainted with crabs. Once, after his ship had been wrecked at sea, he survived for three moons marooned on a rocky isle deserted of everything but a hoard of crabs. Though small, the crustaceans existed in such great numbers on the island that it was a constant battle to keep from being picked to death, piece by tiny piece, by the voracious, unyielding army of the fierce little creatures. However, they did provide him a ready supply of food, without which he would never have survived the ordeal.

Sinbad and Fetu watched in bewilderment and horror as the strange rocks began to lift off the cavern floor and revealed themselves to be not rocks at all, but the speckled grey body shells of giant crabs.

The field of eye stocks sank back down into the huge shells as the things rose from the floor, their numerous armored limbs stretching out from beneath their bodies.

The things were about the size of men, but there was something else besides their size that separated these things from ordinary crabs.

After their extended legs lifted their shells from the floor, Sinbad observed that, unlike crabs, these creatures' body shells were long and roughly rectangular, as opposed to wide ovals, and each shell was curiously segmented about midway down their backs. The segments flexed as they rose, and half the length of their shells bent upwards, leaving flat the sections with six of their ten alien legs. Those six legs carried the creatures about in a decidedly crab-like locomotion, as the raised segments stood straight up and exposed the thick, ribbed armor plate that covered their chests and guts. The creatures' formerly extended eyes had pulled back into large bulges protruding from the tops of their shells, giving the impression of helmeted heads. The four arms protruding from the creatures' upright torso segments, including two that terminated in massive claws, stretched out wide and then quickly flicked in toward their chests, grasping at the air in front of them and pulling it in.

There was also some horrifying suggestion of men in their forms. Were these creatures the ghastly result of the Master's sorcery—once men, now half way transformed into crabs—or were they crabs on their way to becoming men? To Sinbad, it didn't matter if the blasphemes against sanity had been created in one terrifying moment of magic when men mingled with crabs, or if they resulted from a slow, inexorable transmogrification. Being as large and numerous as they appeared to be, if they fought as fiercely as their tiny island cousins, he and Fetu were in for the fight of their lives.

Perhaps he and Fetu would end up like these creatures, Sinbad contemplated for an instant. Was breathing the vile cavern air enough to condemn them to this fate?

Before Sinbad or Fetu could express their shock at the sight, the creatures began closing in around them, frantically clicking with agitation and swinging their jagged and pointed arms. Aside from the clicking, the only other sound the creatures made was the sharp, hollow clacking when their huge claws opened and then clamped shut.

"Oh, this gonna be big fight, Captain." Fetu stated the obvious.

"We can't retreat, there are too many coming up the tunnel. We need to get out of this cavern!" Sinbad yelled as he jumped forward and commenced the battle.

His scimitar batted away one of the creature's jabbing, pointed arms, but the blade didn't slice into the thick shell. With all his might, Sinbad thrust his sword into the creature's gut, but its stout armor again stopped the blade.

Fetu, with his exceptional strength and massive scimitar, was having less difficulty injuring the attacking monsters. The powerful strokes of his huge blade sheared clear through the creatures' shells, leaving the severed torso segments to fall limply onto the cave floor. One after another, the crabmen were sliced asunder by the giant, their bodies crashing to the stone as others clambered over the hacked shells to join the fray.

Sinbad took a gory wound to his thigh as a pointed leg with serrated teeth running down its length jabbed him. With four attacking arms, these creatures were formidable foes, and Sinbad knew conventional fighting with his scimitar wouldn't protect him. One creature's massive claw clamped down painfully on Sinbad's left forearm, and blood was flung onto the sand as he fought to free himself. Sinbad swung his scimitar, and the blade came down on the fleshy joint where the armored arm met the creature's body shell. The beast's whole arm was cleaved off, but its claw remained clamped to Sinbad's arm, and only with an excruciating tug did the thing come loose from the bloody wound.

Sinbad ducked and weaved behind and around stalagmites, trying to keep away from the monsters, but the agitated hoard swarmed in great numbers. Sinbad knew he couldn't take many more wounds like the ones he'd already suffered, but at least he had identified a way to injure the creatures.

Sinbad also noticed the floor was strewn with the dried-out shells of dead crabmen, and he slipped his injured left forearm into one of the hollow arm segments, providing him a protective gauntlet to knock away the attacking arms as he hacked them off at the creatures' joints, sometimes severing two arms with a single stroke. But the swarming monsters were numerous and, riding their six-legged bases like bizarre ocean centaurs, the things crowded in around him.

"There are too many of them!" Sinbad yelled as he hacked off another creature's menacing pincer. "We must flee!"

Sinbad scanned the cavern and spied another natural tunnel intersecting the large cavern about ten men's height up the steep wall. He imagined their only chance for survival was to get up the cliff and into the cave, hoping the wall would be too steep for the crabmen to climb.

"Into that tunnel!" Sinbad announced his plan for escape.

"Aye, Captain!" Fetu answered, and he flashed his forbidding tribal glare.

Fierce war cries echoed through the cavern, and the severed body parts of crabmen went flying, their alien entrails painting the cavern floor yellow and green on either side of the smiting island warrior as he hewed a path to the wall.

As he ran, Sinbad tossed the shell from his injured forearm and slipped his scimitar under his belt. He jumped up onto the cavern wall when he reached the rocky cliff face and began frantically scrambling upward.

As Fetu reached the wall, he gave one last mighty swing of his scimitar to clear the swarming creatures and give himself an instant to begin the treacherous climb, but the crabmen were immediately back upon him, attacking with their jabbing and pinching arms. Fetu hadn't time to slip his scimitar through his belt, and he would definitely need both hands for the climb, so, with a wide, easy swing of his arm, he pitched his sword into the air as he jumped up onto the wall. The massive blade flew up in a gentle arc, passed Sinbad as he climbed, to land softly in the mouth of the cave above.

But Fetu hadn't yet climbed out of reach of the creatures' arms, and one giant claw bit at his leg while another clamped shut with a bite of his tunic and belt. The creature began pulling heavily on his belt, and Fetu strained to keep hold of the wall as the thing tried to pull itself up. Another crabman tried to climb up the shell of the one that had locked onto the belt, and Fetu's face showed the great effort he was exerting to stay on the wall. But the creature's claw was secure, and something had to give. Fetu's massive shoulders ripped through the top of his tunic, and an instant later, both the fabric and belt were torn from his body, leaving Fetu clad only in his loincloth, but free of the pincer. Sinbad stretched out a hand to help him up over the edge, and they both looked down to see the cavern completely filled with the strange clicking creatures. Thankfully, the wall was too steep for the crabmen to climb up after them.

"They be very hungry," Fetu nonchalantly observed.

"There may be a passage for them to get up here," Sinbad warned as he scanned the floor, looking for their tracks. He found none, but he was still wary. "We should get moving."

Sinbad removed his ripped shirt and fashioned bandages for his and Fetu's wounds as the men cautiously continued into the dim tunnels.

They passed through other large caverns and intersecting tunnels, climbing up the innards of the island under the great palace. They followed a definite path, albeit long disused, cut into the stone floor by heavy foot traffic some time ago.

What dangers may lie ahead, they could only guess, but all the passages were devoid of any crabmen.

As they continued groping through the confusing maze of dark caverns, Sinbad feared they could become forever lost in the stony labyrinth. The dim remnants of sunlight that had filtered through fissures in the mountain rock and lit the lower caverns faded away as they proceeded. Given how much time they had spent traversing the caves, Sinbad figured it must be nearing midnight. They could no longer hope for daylight to even partially light their path.

Eventually, the rough natural tunnels led to a steep staircase cut out of the solid rock. Large, curious gemstones, widely set in the walls, eerily glowed, the faint luminescence providing just enough light to traverse the treacherous, slimy steps. Up and up they climbed, cautiously moving into the bowels of the palace above.

In time, they climbed to a point from which they could see a spot of light far above at the top of the winding stone steps. Whomever this "Master" was, and whatever terrible magic he controlled, they would likely soon find out.

At the top of the staircase they found a long corridor constructed of massive stone blocks and lit by ornate gold oil lamps. Each of the lamps was a priceless treasure, and Sinbad and Fetu marveled at the wealth that just one of the lights would bring if they could abscond with it. Along one wall of the passage were huge iron doors spaced about fifty paces apart. All of the doors they passed were shut tight and locked until they came to one that was wide open.

Inside the door was a long, empty corridor, dimly lit by more gold oil lamps hanging from chains affixed to the walls. There didn't seem to be any other doors or connecting passages in the hall, but it was so long that what lay at the other end was out of sight.

As they entered the wide doorway and cautiously moved into the long corridor, Sinbad and Fetu were startled by the squeaking of rusty hinges and a loud clanging of iron behind them. They both wheeled to see the door they had passed through had been slammed shut. The handleless barricade was locked closed with no apparent way to reopen it.

As the two men inspected the door, searching for some release mechanism, they were hit by an instantaneous wave of cold air. When they both wheeled back to look down the corridor, the men stood wide-eyed in shock as they tried to make sense of what they were seeing.

They now looked down a wide tunnel whose only similarity to the corridor they had entered was its extreme length. Every other aspect of the space had inexplicably altered.

"Captain, what be real here?!" Fetu's breath was puffs of steam.

"We're trapped in a hall of illusions," Sinbad whispered in horrified amazement.

Whether illusion or reality, they were now at one end of a misty tunnel that was frozen like a northern winter. The icy walls of the corridor rose up to a tall, arched ceiling in which large circular openings were cut into the chamber above at about every thirty paces. Through these, a weird light shone down into the tunnel and illuminated wide round pits of varying diameter that lay directly below many of the gaping holes in the corridor's ceiling. The tunnel was also lit by a dozen large torches periodically set in mounts along both walls.

Although the tunnel was frozen, it was obvious to Sinbad that this was also a place where great fires had burned. In the ice that was built up around the rims of the dark, stinking pits in the floor were piles of strange, chimeric bones. It looked to Sinbad as if the hacked and scorched carcasses had been disposed of in the chamber above and were meant to fall down the bottomless pits, but some of them had missed the holes and landed around their boundaries. These pieces of unholy corpses, in various stages of decay, seemed to be impossible combinations of creatures and men, not unlike the crab-things they had fought earlier. There were bird-men and reptile-men, and other forms that Sinbad couldn't identify, but one thing was easily recognizable: many wore sailor's earrings like the ones in Sinbad's ears.

"We must find the crew before they suffer this fate," Sinbad whispered uneasily.

"Aye," Fetu agreed, horrified by the sight of the frozen dead things.

As they proceeded down the hall past the pits and piles of frozen body parts, the Master's misty servant materialized at the far end of the corridor next to a massive, rough block of ice that stood atop a wide stone pedestal. Inside the frozen block, something huge and dark was encased, trapped by the ice and awaiting release.

Floating in the air near the top of the block, the imp, with a single tap on the ice from its tiny vaporous finger, started a dreadful process that would further shake Sinbad and Fetu's perceptions of reality.

From the point at which the imp touched the ice, cracks raced down the block in a web of jagged, glittering lines. When the cracks reached the stone pedestal, the entire corridor began transforming yet again.

Like a disturbance rippling across a pool, down the hall rolled a wavefront of thawing illusion that metamorphosed the tunnel from one of cold and ice into one of dank heat, thick with the smell of rotting flesh.

"Captain, what bad mana do these things?" Fetu inquired. Sinbad had no answer but a shake of his head.

They both stood frozen for a moment, staring down the corridor, expecting another sudden change in the environment, but none occurred.

With his eagle eyes squinting into the dim distance, Fetu gave an encouraging assessment.

"Fetu see nothing to fear here."

At that instant, huge chunks of ice began breaking from the cracked block at the far end of the tunnel, and the mysterious dark thing at its center started becoming exposed. The top of the block broke apart, and the head of some massive creature shook off the ice shards and screamed a ferocious roar that echoed down the hall. The thing threw its arms wide, shattering the rest of the ice, and the creature leapt down off the pedestal and came barreling down the dungeon tunnel.

"*That* has the look of something to fear," Sinbad bewilderedly warned.

Although the thing was too far down the tunnel to fully identify, Sinbad thought he recognized its distinctive gait. On one of his voyages to the dark continent that lay far to the south, he had seen such creatures in the wild. The thing charging down the hall appeared to be some kind of gigantic ape covered in thick, dark fur, its powerfully muscled limbs propelling it at a great speed. The monster huffed and snorted in agitation as it charged, and occasionally between steps, it reared up and beat its chest with its massive, flailing arms in a threatening gesture.

"Maybe Captain let Fetu say hello to big monkey, eh?" Fetu said as he stepped forward.

Fetu stood at the center of the corridor, holding his massive scimitar down at his side. Now clad only in a loincloth and strapped sandals, his massive, muscular form, together with the giant sword, presented an astounding aspect of barbaric power. The swirling lines of the tattoos covering his skin rippled with the flexing muscles beneath as Fetu calmly walked down the corridor toward the charging monster.

Sinbad hadn't notice before, but with most of his tattooed skin now visible, when Fetu passed into darkened areas of the tunnel, the beautiful, intricate patterns that shaded many parts of his body made his silhouette break up and disappear in the faint light, with the more visible un-inked skin leaving the impression to the beholder of a stylized skeleton burning with spiky flames. Sinbad could only see his giant friend's fantastic appearance from behind at that moment, and that visage was bizarre and terrifying enough. What madness in men would come from a look at Fetu as he approached carrying his giant scimitar, Sinbad marveled. But whatever sight it might be to a man, Sinbad knew the monster charging down the corridor likely wouldn't even take notice.

When Fetu reached one of the areas illuminated by the eerie light falling from the chamber above, but where there was no gaping pit, he stopped strolling and awaited the beast in the circle of light.

So fantastic was the sight of the sword-wielding warrior lit from above and the charging monster bearing down, that Sinbad imagined he was about to witness an age-old primordial conflict between man and beast.

When the creature had closed half the distance of the tunnel, the strange light shining through the holes in the ceiling suddenly faded away, leaving the tunnel illuminated only by the torches on the walls.

Now that the creature was nearer, when it passed in and out of the torchlight as it charged down the corridor, Sinbad could clearly see it was some unholy mating of creatures akin to some of the rotting bones in the tunnel, only this thing was considerably larger.  It did have a body similar to the powerful giant apes he'd encountered, but Sinbad could see its head was something not of this world, apart from dark magic. The thing looked to have bull's horns.

As it closed in, the monster suddenly began bounding about in the tunnel, weaving back and forth around the pits as it charged.  As the horned ape-thing flew by the last pit separating it and Fetu, the creature stretched out an enormous hand and grabbed one of the giant torches from the wall.

Now Sinbad could clearly see the thing's unbelievable features.  Out of the sides of the giant ape's head protruded thick horns in some ways similar to those of a bull.  The dark spikes came straight out the sides of the creature's head at the top of its tall, sloped forehead.  The ribbed horns then swept elegantly down and forward, ending in two sharp points at eye level that extended a foot's length in front of the monster's face, pointing directly forward on either side of the beast's single giant eye.  Set in the center of its wide forehead, the eye resembled that of a lizard or perhaps feline, with a narrow vertical pupil.  This creature did indeed seem to be a melding of different beasts; perhaps one of its parents was from the race of one-eyed giants Sinbad had previously encountered. Its hulking body bore numerous scars, and Sinbad wondered if it was yet another discarded blasphemous experiment like the ones whose bones littered the corridor, but one that had survived the abominable ordeal. Perhaps most disturbing of the details Sinbad noticed in this short moment of observation were the attributes of the beast's face. It was definitely a face with elements of ape and bull, but was there also the faint aspect of a man?

As it bolted forward, the creature roared something seemingly almost intelligible in an inhuman, guttural voice. To Sinbad, it sounded like the monster screamed: "Blood!"

Fetu matched the monster in kind, screaming a deafening war cry as he lunged forward, and the two forces of nature joined in battle.

The monster swung the massive flaming torch like a club, and Fetu met it with a two-handed swing of his giant scimitar. Firey embers burst in the corridor as the blade sheared off the burning end of the torch, leaving the monster holding what was left of the shaft.

Not wanting the shame of standing idly by and watching while his friend fought alone against the beast, Sinbad jumped into the melee and slashed with his scimitar, slicing into the monster's gut.

The thing screamed in raging anger, and with a buffet from the back of its huge club-like fist, Sinbad was sent flying across the tunnel to slam into the far wall.

The horned cyclops then turned its attentions back to Fetu, and it swung the stump of the torch at the island warrior. Fetu again yelled furiously, and met the monster's attack with another swing of his scimitar. The severing resulting from this stroke was the creature's arm at the elbow.

Blood gushed from the stump, and the monster grabbed at the gory, spurting remnant of its arm with its remaining hand. It roared again, this time with as much pain as anger.

Despite its severe hurt, the beast was not deterred from the fight. It ducked its head and jumped at Fetu, its massive horns leading the way. Fetu lunged to meet the creature with his giant scimitar raised above his head, his powerful muscles flexing into knots with the force of the impending cut. The brutal collision of the blade coming down on the top of the creature's skull was the first contact between the combatants in this round of the fight. The sword-swing was a brutal attack, but the bone of the monster's head was thick, and it stopped the blade from inflicting injury beyond a gash in the thin flesh covering the top of the creature's skull. Fetu's strike did, however, deflect the monster's head down, knocking its deadly horns away from his gut. As he tried to jump clear, the beast rammed Fetu in the thigh, goring him with one of its sharp spikes. The creature then violently jerked its head back, flinging the giant man into the air like a rag doll. Fetu crashed to the floor behind the creature, and his scimitar clanged as it hit the stone and skidded into the shadows. The monster, again clutching at its spurting stump, turned to Sinbad and narrowed its massive eye. Over heavy breaths, it rolled a low growl of malevolence.

Sinbad quickly inspected the tunnel, looking for his scimitar, but when he was thrown across the corridor by the monster, the sword had flown somewhere out of sight.

The beast launched at Sinbad in a hobbling charge on its three remaining appendages, again leading with its curved horns like a rampaging bull. Sinbad backed against the tunnel wall, frantically scanning the area for anything that might be used as a weapon. The monster huffed and panted aggressively as it barreled toward Sinbad, who could find nothing to battle the creature with; that is until the flickering torchlight caught his eye.

As the monster closed in, Sinbad pulled a huge torch from the wall and lunged to meet the charging beast. Sinbad thrust the flaming torch, jabbing the creature directly in its wide alien eye. The collision knocked the torch from Sinbad's hands, and he was thrown back against the tunnel wall, but the deadly sharp tips of the creature's horns hadn't pierced him.

The monster reeled backward a few steps and howled in

pain as smoke, stinking of burned hair and flesh, rose from its head. It blinked its massive eye frantically as it tried to shake off the injury, and after a moment, it had again fixed its cyclopean gaze on Sinbad. The thing ducked its head, and put its single giant hand on the floor, preparing for another charge.

But at the instant the monster launched toward Sinbad, its narrowed eye widened in surprise. Fetu had jumped onto the beast from behind and locked his arms in a death grip around the ape-thing's massive neck, yanking its head back. The monster staggered backwards with Fetu riding its back, pawing at him with its one hand. The beast swung its head back and forth, trying to dislodge the giant man, but Fetu's grip didn't waiver. The monster roared as it wildly stumbled about the tunnel, seemingly choking and gasping for air, and Fetu rode the beast like a bucking stallion, never loosening his hold and all the while yelling triumphant war cries.

For a moment, the two combatants were locked in the deadly wrestling match, whirling and jumping back and forth down the tunnel until finally the heels of the monster caught the raised stone rim of one of the wide pits in the center of the corridor.

Down into the dark abyss they both tumbled, Fetu screaming over the monster's roar.

"Captain!"

"Fetu!' Sinbad cried as he rushed up to the edge of the pit. There, only darkness and silence met his senses. There was no sign of Fetu or the beast, and not even the faintest of sounds came up the wide hole.

"Fetu!" Sinbad again called, but no response came.

Sinbad was left standing alone at the edge of the pit in the now quiet corridor.

After a moment inspecting the pit, Sinbad could see there was no way to climb down, and he realized that if he wanted to determine Fetu's fate, it would be by another way.

Just as Sinbad collected his scimitar (which had slid out of sight behind the raised edge of the pit) and turned to look down the corridor, another wave of illusion rolled down the long hall from the far end.

It suddenly occurred to Sinbad that perhaps the fight with the ape-beast and Fetu's fall were the illusions, and what he saw at that moment was actually real.

Whatever the truth, Sinbad now stood in a tunnel that was again frozen and icy.

When Sinbad had finally crept all the way to the other end of the long, frigid tunnel, he found three unlocked doors and   proceeded through one.   Apparently whatever had trapped the two men in the corridor never expected either one to make it to the end.

The passage eventually ended at a wide stone stair that led up one level and opened into a perpendicular hallway. As he cautiously approached, Sinbad was startled by the sudden appearance of a long shadow moving down the passage at the top of the steps.  He ducked into the shadows at the side of the hall and observed.

A moment later, a man passed down the corridor.  It was another ensorcelled servant of the Master, brother to the ones in the Golden Marlin.

When he could no longer hear any activity, Sinbad crept up the stairs and peered into the passageway.  Down the hall in one direction he saw other servants moving passed in another intersecting tunnel, while in the other direction he saw nothing but an empty passage, but from which he heard faint yells emanating. Were these the defiant screams of as-yet-unmesmerized men? Were they the voices of his crew? Sinbad stealthily moved down the passage toward the noise.

Through an open door, Sinbad again heard a burst of aggressive yelling, and this time he was sure he recognized the voice of his first mate, Ali. The guard at the door stood up at hearing the commotion and walked out of sight into the dungeon.

Sinbad quietly rushed up the passage to the open doorway and edged his eye around the corner. The long corridor lined with cell doors convinced Sinbad that this was in fact the castle's dungeon. A moment later, the single guard reappeared in the hall, returning to his post. Sinbad waited in the shadows with his scimitar in hand.

Aside from the thick, cracking clunk the man's severed head made when it hit the stone floor, Sinbad dispatched the servant as silently as would have the Thief himself. Sinbad collected the ring of cell door keys from the body before dragging it out of sight.

He proceeded down the corridor, peering through the small barred windows in the thick wooden cell doors, searching for his crew. After passing by a few empty cells, Sinbad inspected yet another and his heart leapt for joy upon the sight of familiar faces, alive and as yet unmolested by the Master's sorcery.

"Can I repay you a favor?" Sinbad whispered with a smile while jingling the keys to the dungeon.

Naseem, the Thief of Baghdad, stood just inside the cell and the forlorn look on his face melted into a grin.

"Captain! How did you find us?" he whispered in amazement.

Ali and the other crewmen rushed to the cell door and crowded around the tiny window as Sinbad searched for the correct key that would release them.

"Where are we? How did you get here, Captain?" Ali and the others murmured as they exited the cell.

"There's no time to explain it all." Sinbad hushed the

men. "We are in the dungeon of the Master's palace," he explained. "How many of the Master's servants have you seen? Do you know where they're barracked?" Sinbad inquired of Ali.

"We've only seen a few of the guards, all of them ill with some fever," Ali related. "They all come from down that hall." He pointed back toward the tunnel Sinbad had entered through.

"Ali, you must find a way out of the castle. Take the men and make your way to the north end of the island. There you will find a ship with which we can escape. Ready her to leave," Sinbad ordered and Ali nodded. "Naseem and I will rescue the princess and meet you there. It must be nearly sunrise by now. Flee the island before midday, with or without us. If we haven't met you by then, we'll not be coming at all," Sinbad fatally explained.

The two groups split, Ali and the crewmen heading out the way Sinbad had entered, as Sinbad and Naseem continued into the bowels of the palace.

Sinbad and Naseem hadn't gone far before the Thief stopped the captain in front of one of the small alcoves that were periodically built into the sides of the passage.

"What is it?" Sinbad whispered with curiosity.

"I see a thief's handiwork here," Naseem said as he ran his hand up and down the carven ridges framing the alcove.

An instant later, the Thief had opened a secret door concealing a low, narrow passage behind the alcove.

After closing the panel behind them, Sinbad and Naseem began to explore the hidden tunnels. It was soon obvious that a maze of secret passages was built within the castle, passing by countless chambers where small holes or gaps between stones allowed for a covert view into the palace spaces. Some of the tunnels passed above the chambers, giving Sinbad and Naseem a view down into the wide rooms and halls, while in other places the tunnels skirted along and around chambers at the same level, where secret panels opening into the rooms lay hidden, disguised amid the carven stone walls. Whatever purpose the secret passages may have once served, the dusty, long-untrodden floors in the tunnels suggested they had been empty of any activity for years.

As they continued to secretly move through the lower palace, one view through an observation hole was of particular interest to Naseem.

"A den of dead dogs," Naseem whispered as he gawked through the tiny hole.

The Thief looked down into one end of the main barracks where the Master's ensorcelled servants rested. The lethargic guards lay on rugs that lined the sides of the long, high chamber, and braziers scattered amongst them poured strange smoke around the mesmerized men. In most ways the pitiable souls they looked upon were already dead, only persisting through some dark magic in the smoke. The sharp, acrid fumes even seeped into the secret passage, and Sinbad and Naseem had to move on before the noxious stench overpowered their senses and put them in the same sleepy state as the servants.

Finally, at one secret door, the Thief's intuition and the view into a small, unoccupied chamber convinced Naseem this was a safe place to explore. It was also not insignificant that a gleam of gold caught his eye through the peephole.

Sinbad slipped the scimitar from his belt and readied himself for whatever they might find.

A stone panel slid back, and Naseem and Sinbad stealthily hopped down to the floor of what was some kind of wizard's workshop and necromantic machine maintenance area. Sinbad recognized copper-and-gold tubing and gold gear assemblies identical to some he had seen inside the heart of the Golden Marlin. He also recognized a portable rack loaded with six of the gleaming gold canisters Sinbad knew contained an entire cloud of potent sleep-inducing gas.

Naseem was already in front of the impressive treasures before Sinbad could even mention the curious objects. The Thief's wide-eyed gaze flashed back and forth across the long tabletop covered in wizardly treasures, only stopping momentarily to prioritize his list of things to acquire when the time came.

"These gold canisters hold the green mist that put us to sleep," Sinbad explained.

The cylindrical containers, about the size of a goat's head, were sealed by a wide seam that pinched two cup-like halves together. One of the canisters was among the items Naseem quietly slipped into his shirt and trousers.

After a quick inspection of the chamber, Sinbad peered out the door to the corridor outside and, hearing the sounds of stirring guards not far down, he concluded they were still too close to the servants' barracks to start an exploration of the palace; they could get caught amongst too many of them to escape. He believed the best course of action would be to continue down the secret passages until they reached the Master's chambers. But Naseem had another plan.

"If my captain wishes, I think it prudent to ensure we never have another sight of those rotting men."

Sinbad cocked his head and squinted his eyes inquisitively. Naseem explained.

"If we find the princess, we must still escape from this castle and get off the island. Those dogs are sleeping now, but if they are roused by the Master's magic...we won't want them running down our backs as we flee," Naseem reasoned.

Sinbad nodded.

"Allah willing, we'll make it off this accursed isle," he prayed.

"'Trust in Allah—but tie your camel tight.'" Naseem winked.

Sinbad grinned.

"Alright, but how do you hope to slit so many throats before it's your own that's cut?"

"I'll let sleeping dogs lie," Naseem whispered through his grin of devious plans as he pulled from his billowy shirt the gold gas canister.

Sinbad smiled and nodded in agreement as he understood Naseem's plan. Sinbad had noted that the servants in the Golden Marlin had taken care to avoid the gas, so it must still be poison to them even in their ensorcelled state.

"Very well," Sinbad agreed. "I'll follow the secret passage into the inner palace to find the princess. When you've sung your lullaby, come to meet me there," he instructed.

"Yes, Captain, but please be careful. People who spoke of the Master were crippled with fear of him," Naseem warned. "Trust in Him, but fear those who do not fear Allah," he bade Sinbad, who grimly nodded.

"I trust that this blade will stain as red with wizard blood as would it pig," Sinbad sneered, holding up his scimitar before slipping it back into his belt.

Sinbad's expression lightened.

"You're quite the philosopher. Did you thieve a tome of proverbs?" Sinbad joked.

They both had a hushed laugh before Naseem opened the secret panel, and both men squeezed back into the hidden passage.

They clasped their hands heartily and, after giving each other a nod, they turned and shuffled off down the narrow passage in opposite directions.

Eventually, Naseem made it back down the passages to the servants' barracks. A view through the peephole showed not much had changed since he had last looked into the chamber. Most of the servants still lay catatonic on the rugs with just a few dazedly moving about.

Naseem moved down the passage to a secret door that opened into the corridor outside the barracks. Before exiting the hidden tunnel he wrapped his sash around his head, covering his mouth and nose in an attempt to keep as much of the vile smoke out of his lungs as was possible. He then cracked open the secret door and peered out to ensure the coast was clear.

Down the corridor, standing near the open door to the barracks, was a single guard. Naseem stealthily crept into the corridor then slipped into a shadow. When he was sure the guard's attention was elsewhere, he crept closer, again hiding against the shadowed wall.

Out of the darkness streaked a flickering silver flame, and the servant silently fell to the floor, clutching at the dagger transfixing his neck. Naseem was even able to rush up quickly enough to catch the guard's falling spear before it crashed onto the stones. It was another undetected kill for the Thief.

He pulled the corpse out of sight then returned to the barrack door. After tightening the sash over his face he peered into the chamber then quickly slipped in.

The Thief ducked behind a tall gathered curtain whose top was hung near the chamber's high ceiling. And up he went, climbing the stone blocks behind the shrouding black velvet, unnoticed by any guard.

In an amazing display of agility and skill, Naseem silently climbed along the top of the wall like a spider, hanging from the decorative stone molding that ran the length of the tall chamber. When he reached the center of the guards' sleeping quarters he stopped above one of the oil lamps hanging from the wall below him. From his belt he pulled the gold gas canister, and delicately lowered it on a fine cord. Eventually, he gently and noiselessly let the canister come to rest atop the oil lamp, sitting it directly above the small flame. Naseem then quickly egressed from the chamber in a manner similar to that with which he had entered.

He waited in the shadows outside the chamber until a pop from the canister's seam, followed by a constant whistling, presaged the clouding of the barracks with sleeping gas.

Before slipping back into the hidden passage, Naseem closed and bolted the barrack door, trapping the servants and the poison mists inside.

In the secret passages of the upper palace, Sinbad peered through a narrow observation slit and saw a darkened chamber lit by a few scattered candles and some eerie glow, the source of which he could not readily identify. At the center of the room was a low dais upon which sat a kind of altar. Something, or someone, was lying on the dark green slab of stone, but his view was partially obscured by one of the pillars that ringed the dim space. All he could see was the sleeper's feet and the hem of gold thread at the bottom of what must have been a woman's silk robes, all of which was cloaked in slowly building and ebbing waves of glowing witchfire. Could it be the young princess he sought to rescue, Sinbad pondered.

Although the mysterious castle seemed to be strangely deserted of occupants or activity, from the ornate tiled floor and the carven wall panels, as well as its proximity to the citadel's uppermost levels, Sinbad deduced this was part of the Master's palace and not one of the areas used by the servants. Empty aside from the sleeping occupant, the quiet chamber seemed a fine place to covertly exit the secret passages, identify the room's unknown occupant, and begin the search for the magician. If it was not the princess sleeping therein, but some witch-servant of the Master's, he'd lop off the fiend's head so as not to later face her magic.

Sinbad followed the secret passage a short distance until he came to one of the hidden doors that opened into the chamber. Sliding the latch-stone down and to the side, as Naseem had shown him, unlocked the mechanism, and one of the wall panels slid aside. He cautiously stepped onto the tiled floor and, with scimitar raised, stealthily moved from behind the pillar that stood in front of the secret panel.

Immediately, he could tell that it was indeed a woman lying on the dark stone slab, but she was confined beneath some necromantic haze of slowly pulsing waves of light that flowed across her body.

As he crept closer, daggers of shock and disbelief pierced his mind. The woman was definitely the kidnapped princess. It was obvious from her royal robes and jewelry. But this was not the young girl Sinbad had last seen only two moons before at the palace in Baghdad. Under the magic light-cloak that hovered above her, the young princess seemed to be aging rapidly into a mature woman. Whatever vile transformative spell she was under, the person on the altar was no longer a little girl.

Sinbad approached the low dais and ascended its wide steps. He bent over the altar and stared bewilderedly at the sleeping figure. An unmistakable resemblance of relation to the Caliph was evident in the young woman's face. The necromantic glow was not only altering the princess's body, but even her robes and adornments were growing in size and changing in style to suit that of a maturing young Arabic woman of royal blood.

"Princess," Sinbad called in a hushed whisper, but she gave no reaction. He tried to reach out to awaken her, but some unseen force held back his hand. He could not penetrate the magic with flesh or steel.

As he mused over what could be done to help the imprisoned princess, a tiny glint caught the corner of Sinbad's eye. Across the chamber, in a heap of garments that lay piled in a shallow alcove, something was shining gold. Even in the dimly lighted chamber, Sinbad could see the object glimmering like a beacon, calling out to him.

As he moved closer to inspect the dirty, crumpled silks, another wave of shock hit Sinbad. These were the deep red, gold-trimmed robes often worn by Zahra, daughter of Lessor Vizier Kharim Ahmadi, and the shimmer of gold was being reflected by nothing less than the Star of Percepolis, the Caliph's precious stolen ring.

Sinbad pulled the ring from the shriveled, bony finger and held it in his palm.

"This ring will not leave my finger until I am returning it to the Caliph," he swore to himself as he reverently slipped on the treasure.

Sinbad looked down at the pile of cloth and bones.

"A fitting end," he sneered.

Before leaving the chamber to search for the magician, Sinbad returned to the altar and leaned over the ensorcelled princess.

"I will break this spell and return for you, my princess. I promise," he swore to the sleeping beauty.

With his scimitar in hand, Sinbad nudged open the gold-bound teak door. Given what he had already seen on this dreaded isle, Sinbad steeled himself for finding the worst.

Outside the chamber was a wide corridor that bent out of sight as it curved into the depths of the palace. The passage seemed empty of any activity. Brightly lit by more of the fantastic gold oil lamps, the hall was ornately decorated with a mosaically tiled floor and intricately woven hanging tapestries of silk and gold depicting appalling creatures from some necromantic hell. The imagery was unsettling, but the corridor was deserted of anyone or anything that seemed to pose a threat.

Sinbad stealthily crept down the side of the long, curving hall, passing by the eerie images of the embroideries and bewildering carven reliefs of strange idols cut into the red stone walls. He passed wide arched passageways that led off to the dark outer palace, but Sinbad took none of the intersecting corridors, and continued down the main hall that seemed to be spiraling toward the castle center, where Sinbad was sure he would find the chambers haunted by the wizard.

Suddenly, some motion down the hall ahead of him froze Sinbad in his tracks. Something was quickly and erratically flying back and forth in the wide hall, moving toward him. He pressed himself up against the wall and tried to remain out of sight, but it still approached, and after an instant, Sinbad recognized the thing. Whirling and bouncing down the corridor came the Master's vaporous imp. It was then obvious to Sinbad that the little demon had seen him, for the thing stopped in the middle of the hall and cocked its tiny devilish head from side to side, its burning little eyes fixed upon him.

Like a waft of nauseating scent, a strange sickening sensation suddenly overcame Sinbad. He could feel some kind of mesmerism emanating from the imp, probing his mind like foul fingers of witchcraft trying to grab at his soul.

With this, Sinbad also noticed a strange glow which began burning near him, and the corridor wall along which he stood shimmered in the dancing yellow light.

It was the Star of Percepolis, still held tightly on his finger, which was casting off the soothing light as its magic worked to block the imp's attempts at entrancing Sinbad.

The mist-devil, frustrated and confused by the thwarting of its magic, flittered back and forth across the hall. When its foggy form finally settled, it tried again to ensorcel Sinbad, this time by bringing its airy fife to its lips and piping its silent, magic music. But this attempt at witchcraft was also met with a bright glow from the Star, and Sinbad remained unharmed.

The imp's fife dematerialized from its hand, and the menacing entity then stood on its goat-like hooves in the middle of the hall some fifty paces away, staring at Sinbad, its head tilting to and fro. It held out its tiny hand and beckoned to Sinbad, seemingly trying to get him to follow.

The imp whirled and slowly floated away down the hall, turning back frequently to check if Sinbad was following. Sinbad no longer feared the little devil with the protection of the Star, and he knew that the thing would probably lead him directly to the Master. It was time to end this quiet creeping through the dark palace; Princess Aaliyah needed immediate relief from the transmogrifying spell, and Sinbad was ready to confront the magician, whatever their conflict might bring. Sinbad cautiously crept down the corridor behind the beckoning imp, the Star on one hand and his raised scimitar in the other.

After leading a ways down the corridor, the imp suddenly ducked out of sight down the hall ahead of Sinbad. When Sinbad reached that point in the passage, he saw that the thing had flown into an adjoining space.

One side of the corridor opened into a grand circular chamber where a ring of red stone pillars surrounded a wide opening in the tall ceiling. A balustraded second-level balcony ringed the circular gallery, above which rose a high-domed ceiling. Curious glows emanating from around the pillars caught Sinbad's attention. Set all along the curving walls of the lower chamber were dozens of fantastical objects, obviously imbued with magical potency. On a low dais at the center of the chamber sat an ornate golden pedestal, atop which perched the enigmatic black sphere, its reverent position in the chamber obviously denoting it as an object of great import to the Master.

Sinbad looked upon the grand chamber in wonderment, awed by the grandeur of the space. But his distracted astonishment didn't last long. Out from behind the Ebon

Globe stepped a tall figure in black robes. The magician addressed the sea captain.

"You have crossed a great sea of water to find me, Captain Sinbad, but *I* have traveled an ocean of time to arrive," the magician cryptically uttered in a calm, almost meditative voice with alien accent. "The Ebon Globe foretold of your interference." There was some regret in his tone, and as if for reassurance, he stepped nearer the black sphere. "When the incompetent woman failed to end your life, it became clear I would have to deal with you myself. But after my servant locked you and your giant friend in the lower dungeon with the Guardian of the Pits...I admit, I believed my dealings with you had concluded. I am pleased to personally put an end to your interference, with permanence."

"Enough talk!" Sinbad yelled. "Whatever foul spell you've cast upon the princess, remove it now! I demand you release her!" he commanded.

The tuft of tightly curled black beard that dropped from beneath the Master's chin shook as he laughed.

"You can demand nothing, fool!" he snickered as he raised his arm toward Sinbad. "Die," the Master malevolently hissed as his hand contorted with a necromantic gesture.

Sinbad's hand was also up, raised toward the magician, but it was not the hand carrying his blade.

Sinbad knew the secret of calling the magic of the Star. Many times had he heard the Caliph extol the power of protection bestowed upon those wearers pure of heart and deed, and Sinbad had seen what the ring did against the imp's mesmerism. He was sure it would help him against the sorcery of the Master.

As Sinbad held out the ring like an invisible shield, The Star of Percepolis glowed with a scintillant yellow light that flashed and flickered as it repelled the deadly magic that attacked.

The Master's face contorted into angry frustration, and his hand again gestured at Sinbad, but it was obvious his magic was being blocked by the Star. In being truly pure of heart and deed, Sinbad had been successful in calling the deepest magic of the ring.

"Very well," the Master dismissively sneered. "You will become an eternal decoration amongst the treasures in this chamber," the dark magician promised. "You will be contained." And with this declaration, a prison of ice materialized around Sinbad, trapping him alive but confined in a narrow column of hollow space inside the huge frozen block.

The imp, now half earthly in form and half mist, swirled around and up the massive block of ice before flying across the chamber toward the Master. It slowed to hover just above the floor at the feet of the magician.

Through the hazy distortion of his icy prison, Sinbad watched as the Master parted his black robes and revealed not shaded robes beneath, but some abysmal black space. The infinite void therein pulled at the light around its edges as if it were trying to suck this world into itself. The Master's imp seemed particularly interested in the phenomenon, and the creature excitedly whirled toward it. The fog-demon burst into a tiny cloud before falling into the wedge of nothingness, and then the Master's robe closed.

Naseem shuffled down the long, narrow passage, inspecting the tunnel floor for Sinbad's tracks. Eventually, he reached the point where Sinbad's footprints disappeared under a secret door. Naseem stared into the quiet room through the peephole and, just as Sinbad had seen, the curious partially-obscured sight of the princess asleep on the altar met his eye, but no sign of Sinbad or the wizard. Naseem decided to continue further down the secret passage in hopes of locating his captain.

The secret tunnel swept around various palace chambers, each more ornately decorated than the last, all containing evidence of recent habitation.

The Thief located a secret panel at a point where the passageway seemed to open into the upper level of some grand chamber below. As he exited the concealed door, Naseem silently stepped into a narrow walkway ringing the top of a high, vaulted circular chamber. Peering over the low stone railing, he looked down upon the Master's chamber of magic, where the impressive and enigmatic Ebon Globe sat upon its carven pedestal, and a tall, dark figure, which could be none other than the Master himself, stood alongside the black sphere with his eyes closed in meditation and his hands folded in the sleeves of his robes.

Naseem crept along the walkway to get a better look at other areas in the chamber, and eventually his captain came into view. In the chamber below, Sinbad stood trapped at the center of a massive block of ice, seemingly alive, but hopelessly imprisoned.

Naseem slipped his dagger from its sheath, and cautiously peered around a pillar and down into the chamber. The Master was standing with his back to Naseem, and the Thief raised his knife, preparing to let it fly.

Naseem swung his arm with the precise motion of an experienced thrower, and like a flashing streak of silver lightening, the blade flew straight as an arrow toward the black silks covering the Master's back. Naseem leaned over the stone balustrade and watched for the death-strike, but the familiar sight of his dagger hilt sticking out from his enemy's back never met his gaze.

The knife had sung no more of a sound than a faint whisper as it flew, but apparently it was enough to alert the wizard. Or perhaps he had been aware of Naseem's presence all along. Whatever the case, in a flash of motion and a glow of reddish light, the Master moved more quickly than Naseem's eyes could see. The dagger rang as it harmlessly hit the floor and skidded across the stone tiles. The magician had not only moved aside to completely avoid the flying blade, but he also turned his body around, so that now he was directly facing Naseem, still standing calmly with his hands folded. The Master stared up at the balcony with an evil grin across his face as the dark, bare skin of his head dully reflected the glowing sparks and flashing bolts of energy that began flowing over the surface of the Ebon Globe.

In his icy prison, Sinbad could see the Master's focus drawn away from the black orb and fixed on something above. The frozen walls that confined him seemed to momentarily flicker out of existence at the dividing of the Master's necromantic attentions. Sinbad couldn't see the second-level balcony from where he was trapped, but he had a good idea of what had roused the Master. It could be nothing other than the Thief.

The Master sneered as he raised his hand toward Naseem, and the magician voiced an incantation in some long-forgotten language. From his hand shot a thin stream of fire that sprayed up at the balcony then burst in an explosion of flames in the narrow walkway.

But with his dagger's miss, Naseem had ducked behind a pillar, and apart from slightly singeing his hair, the only damage done by the fire was setting alight the rugs and tapestries in the balustraded gallery.

Naseem had many times dealt with magicians and their dreadful magic. He had slipped undetected into their lairs and pilfered their tomes and trinkets, safely making good his escape before witching doom befell him. Naseem wasn't a necromancer, but he knew well the practitioners of the dark crafts, and he recognized the magnificent Ebon Globe as being some heart of the wizard's power.

From his shirt Naseem pulled a curious little object he had acquired in the Master's workshop. Naseem was confident he knew the small paper cylinder's function, and he thrust the sparkling thread hanging from one end into the flames that crackled on a burning tapestry. The fuse sparked and smoked as it quickly burned away, and Naseem shoved the thing between the stone railing and one of the support pillars.

The bomb exploded with a deafening boom, and a weird shockwave flew through the chamber, trailing a huge burst of roiling grey smoke. The blast shattered the railing and sent broken blocks of stone raining down onto the black sphere, and with a stout kick to a cracked pillar, Naseem added to the torrent of falling debris.

The stones crashed down upon the Ebon Globe in a cloud of dust and smoke, but after a moment, when it cleared, Naseem could see the enigmatic orb still sat perched on its pedestal, unscratched.

The Ebon Globe had escaped unscathed, but Naseem's attack sufficiently distracted the Master and occupied his magic long enough to draw its power away from its other foul deeds. Just for a moment, the ice imprisoning Sinbad flashed out of existence, freeing him.

Naseem slipped back into the secret passage and flew down the tunnel toward a junction to the lower level.

Sinbad had spent what felt like hours locked within the ice, and his mind had plenty of time to mull over his predicament. He had studied the dozens of magic items populating the stone ledges and low pedestals that ringed the chamber. He was confident the objects possessed necromantic qualities due to the way they flashed and glowed along with the Ebon Globe as it seethed with its magic. It was an astounding assortment of rings, staves, gems, masks, and even a cloak, almost any imaginable magician's tool, and Sinbad was convinced he recognized one.

On the flat top of a low black stone stood the Call of Mansoor. Sinbad had studied a scroll in the Royal Library that described the object, including a small drawing of the magical instrument. It was a long sorna horn that rose nearly as tall as a man's thigh. Ornately decorated by carven reliefs and precious inlays, a gold mouthpiece capped the narrow neck of alternating wide bands of gold and turquoise, the last of which widened into its impressive flaring ivory bell, wondrously shimmering with white witchfire. Although most of the horn's secrets had been lost with time, it was written that in an ancient epoch the instrument's sound had brought down a mountain upon an evil king's army. The benevolent king who blew the Call of Mansoor was fighting a righteous battle against the forces of darkness, and his pure intentions and just cause summoned the magic of the horn. Although the Call of Mansoor could not kill directly, its power of destruction could be fatally used against enemies, burying them alive, or breaking their weapons, even sinking their ships. But Sinbad did not want to bury or sink; his only intent was the destruction of the Ebon Globe. He had seen from the falling shattered stones that no hammer or maul could take it apart. Only other magic could destroy this wizardry. And Sinbad wanted to discover just how powerful the Master was without the dark magic of the black sphere.

When the explosion of Naseem's bomb rained the broken stones down upon the Ebon Globe, in a reflexive instinct to shield the black heart of his magic, the Master repurposed his necromantic power, drawing it from all other tasks and focusing the entirety of his sorcery on the sphere's protection. The momentary flickering of the frozen walls that confined Sinbad continued escalating until the block of ice vanished completely in a bright flash of white light.

When the prison of ice fell, Sinbad dropped his scimitar and bolted across the chamber toward the Call of Mansoor. The wizard frantically wheeled when he realized what his wavering concentration had wrought. Naseem's distraction had sufficiently weakened the Master's magic just enough to free Sinbad, and now the captain stood, horn to his lips, facing the Master and the Ebon Globe.

"Fool! You cannot overpower the Ebon Globe!" the Master bellowed unconvincingly.

The wizard stood in front of the Globe like a man sitting on a hole in his carpet, and Sinbad was now convinced that the sphere was the cornerstone of the magician's power. Sinbad had crossed paths with wizards before, and he knew they often drew their necromantic power from magical objects, like the ones lining the chamber walls, objects such as the black orb. It had glowed and sparked when the Master attacked him with magic, trying to incinerate Sinbad as Zahra had been; an attack that had been thwarted by the magical protection of the Star of Percepolis. Just as Naseem had deduced, Sinbad concluded that the Ebon Globe must hold the secrets of the Master's power.

Sinbad blew into the horn, and a bright, reedy sound blasted across the chamber. But with this single magical note, destruction was not brought down upon the Globe or anything else. Instead, the only discernible result of the bewitching vibration was the trapping of the Master. He stood bound, as if held in time, his luminous eyes frozen wide with concern.

Sinbad took a quick, deep breath and blew again, but the strange tableau held: the wizard was immovable. The Ebon Globe and its pedestal started to shake perceptibly but no damage was evident.

Sinbad thought back to his studies of the scroll that described the Call of Mansoor. He remembered the full magic of the instrument could only be called by one who opened his soul while playing the sorna horn. It was written that this exposing of one's soul to the horn's magic would burn evildoers trying to summon the power. But like the ancient king who had brought down the mountain, Sinbad's soul and cause were righteous. He had no fear of the magic.

After another deep breath, Sinbad then began to play the most haunting and intense music he could. He was more than capable of coaxing sweet sounds from the sorna, as he had done with other wind instruments many times before. The magical sounds took on a new timbre of power as Sinbad played, and pockets of air in the chamber began to shimmer and glow with blue pulses of light as he sounded the moody tune.

As he continued playing, Sinbad focused his mind on thoughts of love for his family, and memorable times they had spent amongst the sounds of good music. With this new focus, the vibrations shaking the Ebon Globe intensified, and the Master remained frozen, impotent against the magic of the horn.

Sinbad closed his eyes and deepened his concentration, focusing on the idea of the sphere's destruction, affecting a continually building agitation of the Globe.

Even the magic of the Star of Percepolis swirled in Sinbad's thoughts, "pure of heart and purpose" echoing through his mind, and the ring began to glow along with the magic music. The horn and the ring seemed to be forming a synergistic combination of their necromantic power.

Although he kept his eyes closed, and his concentration never broke, Sinbad was startled by hearing the sounds of accompanying instruments suddenly filling the chamber along with the horn's music. At first, it was only a low dammam drum, beating a rhythm under Sinbad's melody, and then it was also a busy doumbek adding to the unseen ensemble.

Sinbad then concentrated on the grand festivities he had often attended at the royal palace in Baghdad as a guest of the Caliph. The large collection of musicians that performed at the events created an unbelievably complex and rich sound that was almost otherworldly. At this point in Sinbad's music-making, unknown instruments, the sounds of which he was unfamiliar with, joined the swelling philharmonia. Sinbad heard the smooth tones of strange stringed instruments that slid and swirled in the air, dancing around his melody like elegant whirlings of sound. And there were drums and brass horns punctuating the rhythms as cymbals and gongs accented over bells that rang through the chamber. The rushing river of melody and harmony, rhythm and counter-point, washed over the sea captain as he spiritedly played the enchanted horn. The wondrous sounds of the music were so sweet and intense that Sinbad felt himself becoming entranced by the exotic magical vibrations.

The chamber started filling with a thick glow that pulsed in blue flames with the rhythms and sounds of the music. The sound from the end of the horn began flowing through the dancing blue-fire air like slow ripples in a pool. Across the chamber the magical music flowed until the dancing fire filled every corner of the space and enveloped everything within it, including the Ebon Globe.  Then the Call of Mansoor was heard.

The black orb began sparking and its transforming surface shook to a blur.  Bolts of lightning struck out from the vibrating sphere and burned the Master, who still stood frozen, staring at the horn player.

Sinbad felt a sudden super-heating of the chamber's air like a flying wave of scorching heat hitting him in the face and bare chest.  The sharp sensation shook him from his trance, and he opened his eyes just in time to see the Ebon Globe burst into a million black shards amongst a blast of sparkling red-and-yellow flame.

The Star shone brightly on Sinbad's finger, creating a protective bubble around him, and neither the shock of the blast nor the flying shards injured him.

Conversely, now unprotected by his magic, the explosive shock-wave threw the Master down the pedestal steps in a barrage of black stone splinters, and the magician slid across the chamber floor like a hurled doll.  But other than the destruction of the orb and the flinging of the wizard, no other violence or damage seemed to have been wrought by the sounding of the Call.  Nothing was aflame and the palace was still standing.  But the repercussions from the dark sphere's destruction were just beginning.

Upon the shattering of the Ebon Globe, the Master's magic, which had for one hundred centuries held his world together, began to unravel.

In the antechamber where the princess lay on the altar, the cloak of necromantic energy that had shrouded her body and precipitated the unnatural transformation, suddenly vanished in a flash of blue light, and there on the dark jade slab lay not a little girl, but a beautiful young woman.

Although the loud blast that had destroyed the orb momentarily deafened Sinbad, the sound that next met his ears dwarfed all he had ever heard before.  From deep within the earth below the castle came a roar so low and loud that the entire island shook with its fury. What in Allah's name could possibly make such an indescribably monstrous noise was beyond Sinbad's imagination.

With the Globe's destruction came the release of the island's weird creatures which had thereto been trapped by the Master's magic. In the long corridor outside the chamber, Sinbad could hear plaintive howls and wails, and furtive shadows darted past the open arched doorways.

The Master was beside himself with apprehensive concern.

"You fool!" he cursed Sinbad. "Do you realize what you've done? You've brought doom upon us all!" the Master howled as he stared down at the countless black stone shards littering the chamber floor. The Ebon Globe, the heart of the Master's power, could never be put back together.

"Doom..." he moaned in a shaky, frightened whisper.

After a moment, the magician suddenly wheeled and ran from the chamber, his black silk robes flying behind him like a cloak of shadow.

The island quaked violently, and the palace started to collapse. Huge stone blocks began falling from the walls and ceilings, and inexplicably, seawater started spraying up through gaps that opened between the crimson slabs of the floor.

Another quake shook, and it seemed the entire island began to tilt to one side.

Suddenly skidding into the chamber came Naseem. The concern written on his face melted into relief when he saw his captain alive and well.

"Oh, praise Allah you're alive, Captain!" Naseem exhaled. "What on earth can make such a noise?" he inquired in disbelief.

"Who can say, but I'm not interested in waiting here to find out," Sinbad asserted as the crumbling castle rumbled. "I'm going for the princess!" he yelled to Naseem over the din.

"Beware, Captain! Frightful creatures are stalking the halls," the Thief warned. "I'll stay here and gather what I can.

Come back through this chamber after you find the princess, and we'll leave together," Naseem shouted as he produced a large, empty burlap sack from beneath his shirt.

Sinbad took up his scimitar and ran out of the quaking chamber as Naseem began stuffing his bag with the Master's treasures.

When Sinbad reached the antechamber where the princess had been imprisoned under the Master's shroud of magic, he was relieved to see the witchcraft dispelled, but shocked by the appearance of the woman who was awakening on the altar. Could this truly be the Princess Aaliyah? Sinbad had seen the girl not more than a few hours before, and while he took note of the necromantic transformation that was progressing, aging the girl with years as only moments passed, here on the alter lay a woman matured to perfect beauty.

"Princess, can you hear me?" he asked of the awakening woman, who blinked her eyes as the bewitching cleared from her mind.

"Captain Sinbad?" she dazedly answered. "What are you doing here?"

"Come quickly, Princess! We are in great danger!" Sinbad warned the groggy woman. "We must flee the palace before it falls upon us!" he urged.

Sinbad helped the princess onto her unsteady feet, and they rushed out of the room and back down the corridor, headed for the Master's magic chamber.

"What has happened?" Aaliyah lethargically inquired. "I remember being brought to a strange island years ago, and then...I was in Baghdad," she finished, confused.

"The magician held you under some spell," Sinbad answered as he warily led her down the hall. "You've been trapped in this hellish castle for the night," he continued.

"One night?!" she exclaimed, rubbing her temples in an attempt to wake her senses. "That cannot be. I'm sure..." the princess's voice trailed off as the overwhelming truth of her ordeal became clearer in her cloudy mind.

The crimson castle cracked and groaned, buckling from

the shaking of the earth, and stone blocks crashed to the floor around them as they rushed down the passage. Seawater flowed down the corridor like a river, and Sinbad and Aaliyah fought against the strengthening current of the rising tide as they made their way out of the wizard's lair.

When they reached the chamber whose floor was littered with the black shards of the shattered Ebon Globe, Sinbad abruptly stopped at a tragic sight.

"Oh, Naseem," he lamentfully sighed.

Sinbad looked upon another example of that which has long been known: a thief's greed is always his undoing. Out from beneath a massive fallen stone block protruded the hands of the Thief, still clutching the strap of his bulging sack packed with pilfered treasures. Dazzled by the wealth of plunder at his fingertips, Naseem had delayed an instant too long under the collapsing castle.

"A thief is a king until he's caught," Sinbad said in wry tribute to his fallen comrade.

The irony was not lost on him as he slung the strap of Naseem's stuffed bag over his shoulder.

The island again shook violently, and more red stone blocks crashed to the floor around Sinbad and the princess, but before fleeing, Sinbad cupped his palms together and scooped up a pile of the black shards that had been the Ebon Globe, and dumped them into the bag. There was also one last treasure Sinbad grabbed before rushing out of the crumbling chamber: the long, ornate horn that had broken the Master's magic, saving his life and freeing the princess. Sinbad would not leave the Call of Mansoor to be crushed and lost forever under the falling castle.

Sinbad and Aaliyah ran north through the flooding corridors of the collapsing palace toward the castle's main gate. Sinbad couldn't fathom how so much seawater could be flowing into the castle this high up the mountain on which it perched. It was yet another mystery of the strange isle and its crimson castle.

With the drowsy woman gripping one of his arms at the elbow, Sinbad pulled the unsteady princess along as he held up his scimitar, ready to fight as he and Aaliyah proceeded, but the palace now seemed devoid of any of the ensorcelled guards. Naseem's plan to gas the men must have been successful. It was yet another debt he owed to the cunning and skill of the fallen Thief of Baghdad.

Strange howls and screeches emanating from the shadows echoed through the dim corridors amid the rumble of falling stone. The ornate gold oil lamps hanging from the walls swung back and forth on their chains, casting dancing shadows down the halls as they ran.

As perilous as their situation was in the crumbling castle, Sinbad had to stop running at the shocking sight that met his eyes in one wide, columnated hall that opened into the corridor. Through the forest of columns set throughout the chamber, at the far side of the grand space, Sinbad could see that some of the eerie howls that echoed through the dying palace were being voiced by the Master. Held upright atop a red stone altar, the dark magician was being constricted by a dozen thick tentacles that seemed to be growing up out of the stone slab. The Master's radiant eyes bulged out of his skull with the pressure, and his agonized screams added to the cacophony of the collapsing castle.

Sinbad had seen many fantastic sights on his legendary voyages, freaks of nature beyond imagination, as well as all the hellish monstrosities born of black magic, strange things he would never forget, but what Sinbad saw next burned into his mind soul-shaking memories like none before.

The carven stone-panel walls crumbled away, revealing wide swaths of mottled green flesh that quivered and slowly pulsed with wide, flowing lines of colors like a cuttlefish.

The altar broke apart as the chamber quaked, and the gigantic tentacles swelled from the floor. The very foundations of the chamber seemed to be formed from the alien flesh.

A thin vertical line of shimmering and twisting mist appeared next to the altar, and after a moment, the tall, sparkling trail of vapor began to expand midway down its length. The center of the misty line pulled open like a monstrous mouth, exposing a black, star-flecked void within.

The massive tentacles that held up the Master twisted until the magician faced the gaping void.

The surrounding walls of trembling, translucent flesh flexed and undulated as colored patterns raced across their surfaces.

As if pushed out through living gelatinous innards, gigantic alien eyes appeared on many of the walls, pressing up against thick, transparent membranes, all their gazes malevolently fixed on the doomed wizard in the clutches of the giant writhing arms.

Sinbad watched along with the audience of giant eyes as the tentacles holding the Master quickly withdrew, leaving the magician hanging in the air by some witchcraft, floating before the field of eternal black stars.

But the punishment owed the Master was not yet complete. Blasting blue flames like storms of hellfire hit the Master from all directions, burning the fire demon half-breed with a heat even his kind could not endure.

The enormous tentacles shot back up and grabbed the incinerated corpse, and with a violent jerk, flung the charred cadaver into the beckoning void. The Master's burned body flipped heels over head into the oblivion, wheeling over and over as it drifted away into the infinite, until the blackened carcass was no longer visible.

The void's black mouth contracted until it was again the floating upright line of shimmering mist, and an instant later, the twisting smoke vanished.

Sinbad realized the castle itself must be some fantastic creature, some colossal thing trapped by the Master and forced to do his bidding.

But beyond that, Sinbad had seen the gigantic monster wield a sorcery more powerful than any he'd ever seen, obviously even much more potent than that of the Master. Perhaps the thing was some strange alien wizard that the Master had tricked and enslaved, or maybe the thing had learned all the Master's magic, and even more, while it lay held down by the sorcery. What a strange turn of fortune for the powerful wizard, Sinbad mused.

Whatever the truth, among all the dangers they might face during their escape, Sinbad now also feared being eaten by the living structure.

Another strong quake of the castle shook Sinbad out of his astonished stupor, and he yanked at Princess Aaliyah's arm to pull her out of a similar state. Neither of them would ever forget the bizarre and horrific happenings they had just witnessed.

Sinbad, already burdened by the treasure bag over his shoulder as well as the Call of Mansoor in one hand and his scimitar in the other, also had to usher along the lethargic princess. The unsteady woman clung tenaciously to Sinbad's arm as she stumbled along, trying to keep pace. She seemed to be suffering from passing waves of delirium, the remnants of her necromantic imprisonment. If need be, Sinbad was ready to throw the princess over his shoulder and flee, carrying her like a sack of wheat.

As they ran through the collapsing corridors, Sinbad noted that he and the princess were always only left with one obvious route of escape, one open passage while the rest fell to ruin, as if the castle was leading them out, trying to hold together until they passed.

Red stone blocks continued crashing to the floor around them as Sinbad and the princess ran down a wide stone staircase that led to the castle's ground level. Through wide open doors across the chamber, Sinbad could see daylight in the distance.

Only one last gauntlet of dangers remained before they could make good their escape from the doomed castle. Tall archways filled with loathsome shadows from which demoniac sounds emanated lined both sides of the long corridor. Sinbad could see strange creatures, now liberated from the confines of the Master's magic, flirting with emergence from the darkness. Sinbad sensed great danger in the hall, but the freedom of daylight beckoned at the other end.

Again, the island's foundations faltered under the strong

quaking, and the floor pitched further. More seawater inexplicably washed out of the archways on one side of the hall and flooded across the floor, carrying all manner of debris within its flow, including some of the smaller creatures that had been hitherto hidden.

"Sinbad!" the princess suddenly screamed.

In a moment of clear consciousness, she cowered at the sight of larger, more ominous creatures that pulled themselves out of the shadows and into the hall. Claws and tentacles clutched at the stones lining the archways, while loud clicks and unnerving screeches echoed amongst the din of the falling castle.

Although he had his scimitar ready, Sinbad knew he couldn't hack his way through all the monsters coming into the hall. He raised the Call of Mansoor to his lips and blew with all his might.

The bright sound of the Call filled the tall corridor, pushing all other sound out of the hall, and blasting bright light into the shadows. The taloned hands and slithering tentacles shot back into the darkness upon contact with the echoing magical vibrations, and a path to the end of the hall was suddenly cleared. Sinbad and the princess flew for their lives.

The light of the Call faded out and again the tall, eerie hall was dark, save for the frame of daylight that was the open doors at the far end. As they ran past the darkened archways, Sinbad saw some of the monsters being devoured by others, and even the castle itself seemed to be consuming the strange creatures.

More falling stones shattered on the floor behind them as they ran, and bright rays of sunlight began beaming through gaping cracks that opened in the collapsing high ceiling.

They sprinted to the end of the hall, and when they flew out the open doors that led to the palace courtyard, Sinbad breathed a momentary sigh of relief. It was his first breath of fresh air since he had entered the reeking caverns under the island, and the sight of the rising sun in the open sky felt like hope compared to the dark confines of the weird castle.

Ahead of them, they still had a treacherous trek through the unknown dangers of the jungle, but at least they were free from the haunted and crumbling lair of the Master.

"The black moat! It's gone!" the princess exclaimed.

Sinbad wasn't sure to what she was referring, but before them, stretching to the wall that surrounded the castle, was a smooth expanse of red stone tilted to one side.

The gates of the castle wall had vanished, leaving a gaping break in the rampart that led out to the steep cliffs that fell down to the jungle far below.

"Can we ride the flying carpet?" the princess inquired as she and Sinbad passed through the opening in the tall wall.

Although she seemed to have shaken off most of the stupor she had earlier exhibited, as with her comment about the moat, Sinbad believed her to still be somewhat delirious.

"I'm afraid our feet will have to carry us, my princess," he gently coached.

The eternal necromantic dusk that shrouded the crimson castle was giving way to a bright sunrise, and below the palace's high mountain pedestal stretched a vast plane of dense jungle laid out like an enormous green carpet covering the island.

A treacherous stair, roughly cut in switchbacks down the cliff face, appeared to be the only way to proceed. Sinbad slipped his scimitar into his belt, freeing a hand to support the princess, and they started down the narrow steps.

It was dangerous and slow going but the difficult climb also presented them with a surprise boost to their morale. About halfway down the cliff, a rough tunnel opened onto the stairs from inside the mountain, and Sinbad could see the tracks of men that had recently exited the cave and continued down the steps ahead. Could these be the tracks of his crewmen, Sinbad wondered and hoped.

His spirits had been buoyed but the distraction from the island's dangers was brief. Another strong quake shook, and the island again fell further to one side. The sudden shift rocked the princess from her feet and she slipped off the steps, screaming in terror as she fell over the edge.

It was an instant of split-second decision for Sinbad, and he reacted with as much instinct as thought. One hand tightly gripped that of the princess, and the Call of Mansoor tumbled out of the other as he reached for a handhold. Rocks rained down from above and pummeled Sinbad, including the hand that anchored him and the princess to the cliff, but his grip didn't falter.

"Don't worry, Princess! I've got you!" Sinbad assured her.

His chest flexed with the strain as he pulled first himself and then the princess back onto the steps. With relief, she wrapped her arms around Sinbad and hugged him for a moment before steadying herself.

"I'm not hurt. We must get off this cliff!" the princess announced before leading the way down the steps, but always still tightly clutching Sinbad's hand.

The bright morning sun was climbing into the sky when Sinbad and the princess had finally clambered down to the bottom of the canted stone steps. At the other side of the boulder-strewn field that lay at the cliff's base stood a surreal forest from a nightmare landscape. The drastic sinking of one side of the island had significantly tilted the island's expansive plateau, creating a sloping jungle floor where there had been flat, and inclining to one side all the once-upright trees.

But whatever dangers may lie ahead, Sinbad knew the stretch of nightmare jungle lay between them and escape on one of the ships; it must be crossed. Sinbad pulled the scimitar out of his belt.

"Thank you for helping me down, Captain. I am in your debt," the princess sincerely professed. "Here, let me unburden you. My weariness has passed. I have the strength," she asserted.

Aaliyah took the treasure bag from Sinbad and slung the strap over her shoulder.

"Are you sure, my princess? The path ahead will surely be arduous," Sinbad chivalrously offered.

"I am sure. I can do it."

Sinbad's look told her he was unsure.

"...and if this bag were hanging around your neck when you had to use your sword to fight anything more agile than one of those trees...you'd be in trouble, and then I'd be in trouble. I've had my fill of trouble. Now, let us waste no time!" she confidently declared with a smile.

Sinbad smiled back.

"Very sensible, my princess."

He took up her hand and led the way across the slope toward the quaking wall of leaning jungle trees.

As they walked, something on the ground caught Sinbad's eye. He couldn't help but lament at the sight of what was obviously a few glimmering pieces of the shattered Call of Mansoor, but Sinbad took heart that his finger still securely bore the Star of Percepolis.

They crossed the field of rocks and started down an old forest path, following the recently-trod trail of footprints. The jungle was now a forest of perils where trees were falling due to the severe slant of the land, and confused animals fled in the chaos, unable to find safety.

There was yet another strong earthquake, and Sinbad wheeled to look back at the burning palace up on the steep crag. Sinbad and the princess watched as the great tower of the crimson castle fell into ruin.

Another deep and deafening roar came from within the island, and an instant later, the castle was rocked by a tremendous explosion that engulfed the entire structure in a gigantic ball of white fire as bright as the sun. The force of the blast sent countless huge pieces of flaming debris hurling through the air in all directions, trailing long arcs of smoke. The burning projectiles landed throughout the jungle, setting the trees ablaze in scattered pockets.

Then yet another ominous sound startled Sinbad and the princess as a great rumble began moving through the forest. It soon became obvious to them that the last strong quake and tilt of the land had caused boulders from a rocky area to begin rolling into this part of the jungle.

Sinbad and the princess ducked behind a large tree, and crouched under its inclined base to avoid the careening rocks.

Bouncing boulders rolled up the inclined trunks of fallen trees and shot off into the forest as if thrown by mangonels. Huge rocks came flying down the slope as others dropped from above. The colliding stones exploded into gravel that flew off in all directions, and Sinbad huddled over the princess to protect her from the barrage.

It wasn't long before the torrent of rocks subsided and they continued through the forest that was now burning with countless fires started by the fireballs that flew from the exploding castle.

They continued down the trail apace, still following the tracks of those who had gone before. Only the most shocking and gruesome of sights could have slowed their progress, and soon just such a sight met their eyes.

Ahead on the trail lay what appeared to be several charred corpses. Upon closer inspection, one of the incinerated men had been a member of Sinbad's crew. The other two, while unknown to Sinbad, were clearly also sailors, likely others that had escaped from the Master's dungeon with his crewmen. But what it could have been that had burned them so, Sinbad could only guess.

They warily passed the burned bodies, taking care to avoid the foul stinking smoke that still rose from the blackened corpses. Continuing down the trail, Sinbad squinted as he tried to identify any danger ahead.

"Did you hear that?" the princess suddenly called out in a concerned whisper.

Before Sinbad could answer that he hadn't heard anything, a sound came that they both definitely heard. It was unmistakably the cry of a baby.

"A baby?" the princess puzzled.

Then came the sound of not a baby, but a young girl crying. At this, Sinbad knew some witchcraft was playing with them.

"Stay behind me," he bade the princess.

The sounds of the child's cry turned into demoniac laughter, and through the leaning trees ahead of them, Sinbad and the princess saw a bright burst of light, and then a column of yellow flames flying above the sloped forest floor. The cackling apparition of fire frenziedly flittered around the trees as it approached, all the while its foul laughter growing in intensity.

Sinbad stepped forward to try and attract the thing's attention and draw it away from the princess.

The flying fire-fiend ceased its agitated careening through the forest and slowed until it hovered some thirty paces from Sinbad.

The flames at the top of the column of fire pulled back, folding open to reveal the nightmare face of the jungle witch. It was the visage of a crazed island woman with burning red eyes bulging from an emaciated, skull-like face. The horrid countenance sat atop the swaying pillar of fire like the head of a giant flaming snake. The outer fringes of the thing's bushy hair burned with blue witchfire, and her maniacal laughing revealed black shark-like teeth.

The witch fixed its gaze on Sinbad and it slowly floated toward him, its laughter transforming into a deranged muttering.

Suddenly, the thing opened its mouth wide, and from it

shot a ball of fire that flew toward Sinbad with the roar of a furnace.

But Sinbad was wary and readied for an attack. He ducked behind a tree and the flaming ball flew past him into the forest, blasting the trees into flames where it hit.

The witch then quickly turned its attention to the princess and the thing flew toward her with its mouth wide open.

Another fireball shot from its mouth and raced toward the princess, and the apparition again let out a sickeningly evil laugh.

"Princess!" Sinbad helplessly yelled.

Princess Aaliyah cowered behind the stuffed treasure bag and screamed as she awaited her seemingly unavoidable fate.

But as the fireball flew, something in the treasure bag started to glow brilliantly. So bright was the light that it could be seen through the burlap fibers of the sack.

Instead of cremating the princess, the fireball rebounded off some invisible protective field obviously created by whatever object was glowing in the treasure bag. Like the first fireball, this one also flew off into the forest and started a raging fire where it landed.

With this, the witch's laughter ceased and its gruesome head rocked back and forth in confusion and frustration as it flicked about its fiery ophidian body like the tail of an agitated cat.

As the thing slowly floated toward the princess, Sinbad bolted from behind a tree, and came at the witch with his scimitar raised high. The witch saw Sinbad's motion, and the thing was startled out of its puzzlement over its thwarted attack. It turned to Sinbad as he approached, and again hideous mirth echoed from its lips. As Sinbad drew closer, the witch opened its mouth wide.

Just before the scimitar came down on the witch's ghostly neck, the thing spit another fireball at point-blank range. But another magical glow flashed in the forest, and the witch's expression turned from one of diabolical merriment to one of shock and surprise.

It was the Star of Percepolis, shining brightly on a finger of the very hand that was bringing down the scimitar.

The fireball was repulsed by the protection of the ring, and the witch's own flames engulfed her just before the blade sent her burning head rolling down the sloped forest floor, leaving a blazing trail behind it. In a flash of light, the flames shrouding the rest of its form were suddenly extinguished, and a grotesque, slug-like body fell onto the carpet of fallen leaves. Glistening with a thick covering of green mucus, the ghastly black thing, as long as a man is tall and twice as thick as his thigh, curled and writhed in violent death throes as one gory, severed end spit and oozed a vile, dark green blood.

Sinbad and the princess fled from the scene as fast as their feet could carry them. As they ran, Sinbad looked back over his shoulder and saw two more of the fire-hags examining the remains of the first. A moment later, the two columns of flame were flying through the jungle, chasing after Sinbad and the princess.

The witches' fireballs flew past them as they ran, and the leaning jungle trees they passed under were already engulfed in the fires set by the castle's fiery destruction, making it a run through hell for Sinbad and the princess.

As the burning witches flew closer, their throws of fire became more accurate. In fact, one hit the princess square in the back, directly where she was carrying the treasure bag, and again she was protected by something that momentarily flashed within the sack. Sinbad could now see it was the shards of the shattered Ebon Globe that were glowing in the bag and protecting against the witches' fire.

Sinbad and the princess broke through the flaming jungle out onto a short, rocky clearing at the top of the precipice that fell to the level of the dock below. Mercifully, the fire-witches seemed confined to the forest, as they ended their pursuit at the jungle's edge.

Although another crude stone staircase led down this cliff as well, it was a quarter of the height of the castle's precipice. Because these steps were cut in one long line, and not switchbacks like the stair before, these steps were actually easier to traverse given the altered arrangement of the land, and Sinbad and the princess flew down them toward one more short stretch of jungle that lay between them and escape.

Down on the docks, Ali and the other crewmen saw Sinbad and the princess fly from the jungle on the plateau above and begin their way down the cliff to the lower land where the ship waited. The crew had also fought the forest's fiends as they fled, and they knew Sinbad and the princess would need their help. The sun's bright light glinted on steel blades as the crew poured over the side of the ship onto the dock.

After reaching the bottom of the steps, Sinbad and the princess ran through the last bit of jungle, following a trail obviously worn by continuous, heavy foot traffic. Sinbad was thankful this jungle floor seemed nearly level, somehow only slightly affected by the island's cant, and he had seen from the plateau above that the docks lay only a short distance away, but the fact that this trail was so well worn made him worry they might find the footprints' makers, for only a few were those of his crewmen. The rest were a collection of prints made by bare human feet, some appearing to be almost skeletal, and other spoor laid by creatures completely unidentifiable.

The trees grew so dense in this jungle that Sinbad often couldn't see more than a few dozen paces down the path ahead as it weaved back and forth around the colossal, ancient trees. Under the jungle's thick canopy, the forest took on a surreal aspect of day mixed with night, the sunlight beaming in from far ahead as an unnatural dusk towered above.

Sinbad and the princess raced down the path toward the daylight until, when rounding another of the massive, eons-old trees, more shocking sights assailed them.

Along the trail ahead, among other obvious signs of a fierce battle, the jungle floor was littered with the hacked, dead bodies of horrific human ghouls. The dead things somewhat resembled the ensorcelled servants of the Master with their malnourished bodies and festering wounds, but these creatures were completely naked with all of their blotchy, pale skin exposed. But the most shocking aspect of their appearance was an unholy drift from human form. Like some of the other horrors Sinbad had seen on the island, these creatures seemed to have undergone a transmogrification that blended their human bodies with those of various animals.

Whatever the creatures were, it was evident they had attacked those who had come down this path earlier, for among the ghoul carcasses were two dead sailors, their bodies mutilated and half-eaten.

Before the grim details of the scene could be processed by their reeling minds, Sinbad and the princess received another shock. Ahead on the trail, several of the ghouls, still "living," seemed to be feeding on the dismembered corpses of some of their brethren.

The princess shrieked as she saw the abominable sight, and Sinbad scanned the dense forest, looking for any others.

Although the island still rumbled with frequent earthquakes, there was a moment of eerie silence as Sinbad considered how best to proceed. The stillness suddenly broke with the sounds of snapping tree branches and a horrific growing chorus of hisses and moans.

Out from behind the trees came dozens of the ghouls, limping and lumbering toward Sinbad and the princess.

These creatures also seemed to be in a permanent trance, like the Master's servants, but their rancid bodies were even more frail, and their features even more grotesque. Some shambled forward on all fours, dragging themselves along on limbs that seemed barely capable of lifting their body weight, while others stood upright like men, but hungrily stared back with large fish-like eyes, or reached out with reptilian claws, beckoning. What kind of degenerate life could still be harbored in bodies this dead, Sinbad could only wonder, for although the Master's magic had been permanently dispelled, these things somehow remained animate.

As the ghouls closed in around them, Sinbad suddenly felt the same dread of overwhelming numbers that he had experienced when seeing the swarming crabmen. He couldn't hope to cut his way through all of the unholy hoard.

Sinbad grabbed Aaliyah's hand, and they ran down the trail toward the ghouls that were eating the carcasses. Sinbad swung his scimitar and one fiend lost its lizard head, while another got a kick in the chest that sent the rotting waif flying.

Just then, the sounds of yelling men broke over the noise of the rumbling island and mob of hissing ghouls. They were the fierce voices of Sinbad's crew, the men armed and ready for a fight as they ran through the jungle into the melee.

The chimeric ghouls moved slowly but they were many. This level of the island seemed to be infested with the things. Perhaps these were servants that had escaped or found themselves lost and trapped on this lower terrace of the island. Or maybe, Sinbad pondered, after exhausting their usefulness, the Master had simply dumped them into this grove of the forest. The servants of the castle may not have been needed as palace guards at all, but instead the captured sailors may have only been abducted and bewitched as fodder for the magician's unholy experiments in melding man and beast. He didn't think the Master's deeds could be more sickening than what he'd already seen, but these creatures turned Sinbad's stomach anew.

The crewmen rushed to Sinbad's side with their blades swinging, hacking at the swarming ghouls that seemed to come from all directions. Scimitars slashed the creatures asunder and their rotting bodies, many hewn in twain by the steel, flopped to the forest floor. A running battle ensued as Sinbad and his crew fought their way down the trail through the clawing, biting terrors.

"Out of the forest!" Ali yelled to Sinbad. "They don't leave the trees!"

They ran like the very fires of hell nipped at their heels, and eventually Sinbad and his crew broke from the jungle into the clearing that led to the pier. The hoard of ghouls was close behind but, like the fire-witches on the terrace above, these creatures stopped at the forest's edge and did not pursue them onto the dock.

The fleeing group rushed onto Zahra's ship, for it was the only sea-worthy vessel at the dock, and the gangplank was thrown aside once everyone was aboard.

"Cast off!" Sinbad commanded, and Ali directed the crew. "Get us off this island hell!" the captain added, and a moment later the ship was free from the dock and moving toward the open ocean.

Only eleven men other than Sinbad had made it through the ordeal. Six of the men had been sailors on Zahra's ship, but with an oath of loyalty to Sinbad, they eagerly joined his rag-tag band. It was a meager crew, but they were enough to sail the ship to safety.

The morning winds were calm, and only eight men could be spared to pull the oars, but the ship slowly distanced itself from the accursed isle.

Behind them, the land continued to quake and break apart. Fires raged in the jungle, and debris from the sinking island was scattered throughout the surrounding ocean.

After a short while, the eagle-eyed man that had climbed to the crow's nest saw a gleam of gold in the distant flotsam.

"Captain! Golden Marlin, ho! Dead astern!" The startling call came down from the lookout.

"Is she closing?!" Captain Sinbad called back.

"If she is, it's very slow. No, Captain! She's barely moving!"

After another few moments with his eye pushed into a spyglass, the lookout called down again.

"Wait! She's moving now! She's closing!" the lookout yelled.

The sinking island was creating shallow swells in the ocean that expanded out in giant rings around the disturbance. The Golden Marlin was apparently riding the front of one of these waves, and the gleaming gold machine was surfing in fast.

"Captain! It's Fetu! Riding the fish!"

Through his spyglass, Sinbad could now see it was indeed Fetu, standing on the head of the fish and waving a wooden plank he was using to paddle the Marlin like a giant canoe.

"Caught you fish, Captain!" a distant voice boomed across the ocean.

He was battered but, unbelievably, Fetu lived, and he had somehow escaped on the now-inanimate machine.

The magnificent Golden Marlin drifted alongside the ship with Fetu standing proudly on the treasure like a mighty masthead, smiling a wide smile, and now wearing naught but the skin Allah gave him.

The crew laughed and cheered as Fetu climbed aboard, amazed by his miraculous survival. The mirth born of their fellow's return, as well as their escape from the wretched island, continued as they went about lashing the giant mechanical fish to the side of the ship.

Behind them in the roiling seas, the last pieces of the listing island were breaking apart. Now the entirety of the island's jungle seemed to be burning, and an enormous plume of smoke was pouring up into blue skies. With one final rumble from the island, Sinbad and the crew watched as the last massive stretch of the burning land mass slid into the ocean as one enormous piece, like a flaming rug sliding off a tilted table, the billowing smoke transforming from black to grey before fading.

All hands on the ship were looking as out of the fading smoke plume flew some large black creature heading in their direction. Everyone watched as the giant bird or bat flapped its huge wings and climbed higher and higher, passing directly over the ship at a great height before disappearing into the distance.

"Another island floating up!" came another curious call from the lookout, shaking the crew out of their amazement.

Fetu flew up to the poop deck for a better view.

"Look, Captain! The island be father of all jellyfish! It be Big Chief Jellyfish!" he exclaimed in amazement.

To the surface of the water rose what appeared to be another island; not an isle of earth and rock, but one of strange, translucent sea flesh. As Fetu identified, Sinbad also noted the thing bore a resemblance to a jellyfish, only one that dwarfed any sane notion of a jellyfish or any other kind of sea creature. The Master had obviously built his island on the back of the creature, trapping it with his magic.

As if in thanks for their part in freeing the monstrosity, the creature slowly undulated part of its gigantic body, and created a deep, easy swell in the ocean that moved toward Sinbad's ship.

"Get us under full sails!   Hard on the oars!" Sinbad ordered Ali, and the first mate barked to his crew.

As the massive swell approached, it pushed the air ahead of it, creating a building breeze blowing in front of the wave. The ship's sails caught the wind and the vessel picked up speed. When the massive but gentle wave arrived, the ship, along with the magnificent Golden Marlin lashed to its side, was lifted into the air and pushed ahead by the huge roll of water. Fetu yelled triumphal cries while he and the rest of the crew clung to the ship as it surfed down the front of the colossal swell.   Before the wave died out and the sea flattened, it had gently propelled them all the way through the calm morning air until the stiff noon winds were up, and the ship continued under full sails, headed to Basrah.

Sinbad pondered over the fact that the wave had pushed the ship in precisely the direction of Basrah.  Was it just a coincidence, or was the creature somehow even aware of their destination?   The gigantic thing had also seemed to hold together the part of the island Sinbad and Aaliyah needed to cross before the land fell into the sea, and it seemed to seek vengeance against its captor once finally freed.  To Sinbad, the conclusion was obvious, if incredible: the creature possessed an advanced intelligence, and perhaps even an ability to know the thoughts of other beings' minds. It was yet another fantastic part of this extraordinary voyage.

Compared with the events of the previous few days, the journey home was agreeably uneventful for Sinbad's ship and crew.

Much to the amusement of the men, Fetu recounted the story of his adventure after falling into the pit with the ape-minotaur.

"Fetu have big fight with monkey-man in belly of whale! Fetu think pit be blowhole of giant whale, so Fetu climb. But whale make big growl, not like taste of Fetu, spit him out."

He roared and then spat, as if expelling something distasteful.

"Whale spit out Fetu and boats and rocks, spit out everything! Then all dark, deep under water, quiet. Fetu think maybe already dead. Then open eyes, see gold shine come up from deep. Only thing shine gold like this be Captain Sinbad's giant fish! This good mana! Fetu swim hard to fish, still no breathe, hold on to fin, and fish pull up and up with Fetu riding, all the way to sun and waves, and

Fetu breathe and breathe again! But now see not whale—it be Big Chief Jellyfish!"

He contemplatively summed up his experiences.

"Fetu go bottom of ocean in giant gold fish, still breathe, fight big crab standing like man and big horn monkey. Then Fetu see father of all jellyfish! Oh, Captain! Now Fetu know —stories are true! Aiyeeeee!!!" he howled in exuberance.

Sinbad smiled broadly and clasped hands with the tattooed giant.

"And now you too are part of the stories, my friend!"

"Aye! Big thanks, Sinbad, captain man!" Fetu's pride was evident.

Aaliyah also expressed gratitude to Sinbad for her rescue. She told of the strange ordeal she'd been through, living life in the Master's magic. Although only trapped for a day, from her perspective, ten years had passed under the spell, but they had been happy times living with her father at the royal palace in Baghdad. The Master's magic had created the illusion of a normal upbringing, indistinguishable from reality to the princess. During her accelerated growth, she had still learned from her tutors, spent time with her friends, and otherwise lived a normal, full life. In some ways, she felt nothing had been lost at all. To her, forfeiting those years of her life was a small price to pay for avoiding the nightmarish plans of the Master.

Their leisurely trip home also afforded Sinbad time to examine the fantastic contents of Naseem's treasure bag. Inside was a collection of jewels and artifacts bewildering to even the worldly captain. Worth more than all the treasure piled in Sinbad's mansion, these gems and trinkets also possessed powerful magic indecipherable to the sea captain. It would take wise seers and learned appraisers to determine the collection's true necromantic and monetary worth, and whatever value the riches held, those of Sinbad's intrepid crew that had survived the ordeal would collect their deserved shares. Sinbad did note one odd thing regarding some of the bag's contents: the black shards of the shattered Ebon Globe had inexplicably turned bone white.

It was not long after the heinous deeds that the palace uncovered the crimes of Kharim and Zahra Ahmadi. Although Sinbad had already fled, chasing after the princess, the Caliph had sent messenger pigeons to Basrah, carrying news of Sinbad's innocence. Once in Basrah, the messages were transferred to specially trained seagulls that set out across the ocean to find Sinbad. One of the gulls eventually found him on Zahra's ship, and Sinbad replaced the tiny note with one of his own before setting the gull free to return to Basrah. Sinbad's simple message read: "Success. Meet in Basrah at new moon."

Three days later, Sinbad sailed his ship into the harbor at Basrah with the magnificent Golden Marlin still lashed alongside. Curious sailors gawked from moored vessels, and astounded civilians ran up and down the docks trying to get a look at the gleaming gold spectacle, shining in the bright summer sun.

The oarsmen on Sinbad's ship gently brought the vessels up alongside the royal yacht where Haroun al-Rashid, Caliph of Baghdad, waited under a fluttering red silk and cloth-of-gold canopy.

Fetu leapt down from the ship onto the Marlin and then up to the royal yacht where he stood motionless like a statued guard. The startling sight of the tattooed giant caused the Caliph to instinctively cower back, and his guards grabbed the hilts of their scimitars. But out from behind Fetu stepped Sinbad, and the contingent on the royal yacht relaxed.

Sinbad salaamed before pulling the Star of Percepolis from his finger. With bowed head, he presented it to the monarch.

"Your ring, my Caliph," he respectfully offered.

"The Star," the Caliph whispered in awe as he took up the ring, tears welling in his eyes.

Sinbad then stepped aside and presented the now-grown Princess Aaliyah.

"And your daughter, my Caliph—the Princess Aaliyah," he said, waving his arm in a respectful gesture of presentation.

There was a look of confusion and shock on the Caliph's face, but it was erased after a moment when Aaliyah flew into his arms.

"Aaliyah?" the Caliph unsurely asked.

"Father!" she cried in comfort and relief as she jumped to the Caliph, who hugged her tightly.

"Do not mourn for me, Father. I have been through a terrible ordeal, but I am well, and happy to be home with you. If it were not for Captain Sinbad, I would not have returned at all," she explained.

The Caliph looked upon Sinbad with regretful eyes.

"Oh, my son, how did I ever doubt you! You have yet again proven yourself a courageous defender of Arabia, and trusted friend to the Caliph. May Allah find you and your wives worthy of all the best!" he praised the captain, giving Sinbad a sincere embrace.

"Hm...how many wives *do* you have?" Aaliyah inquired of Sinbad with a slightly annoyed tone.

"Allah has seen fit to bless me three time so far." Sinbad smiled as he took up Aaliyah's hands in his and looked lovingly into her eyes. "But I am a very wealthy man...I can expect to marry again."

As Sinbad had decreed in the royal throne room, it was not he, but instead Lessor Vizier Kharim Ahmadi who was beheaded for his treason.

Palace guards found the body of Zahra's slave in the shrubs, and through an interrogation, during which the inquisitor applied certain coercive techniques and methods proven useful in extracting truth, the vizier confessed to the theft of the Star, as well as to what he eventually discovered about his daughter's kidnapping plot, all of which had been orchestrated by the Master and enabled by his evil magic. Kharim Ahmadi paid for his treachery at the following sunrise.

As reward for his courage while falsely accused, and for the return of his precious daughter and ring, the Caliph bestowed the honorable title of satrap upon Sinbad, making him lord of the Baghdad district in which he resided.

It took fifty men and ten camels pulling on the ropes to lift the magnificent Golden Marlin out of the harbor. The fantastic machine, one of the most spectacular treasures in all of Arabia, was moved to the courtyard of the royal palace in Basrah, where its wonders delighted all who came to behold them.

Wise men from around the world came to study the curious mechanism, but for all their exceptional intellects and prodigious bodies of knowledge, none could decipher the mysterious secrets of the Golden Marlin. If it were to ever swim again, it would not be until another transfusion of some magician's necromantic blood made the giant fish's mechanical heart beat anew.

www.ingramcontent.com/pod-product-compliance
Lightning Source LLC
Chambersburg PA
CBHW051300170626
46809CB00004B/1739